P9-DGT-977

You Know Who Killed Me

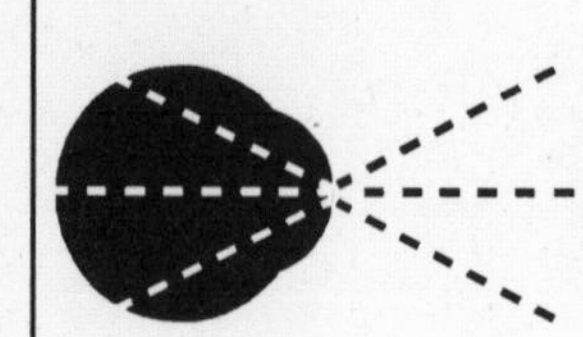

This Large Print Book carries the Seal of Approval of N.A.V.H.

AN AMOS WALKER NOVEL

You Know Who Killed Me

Loren D. Estleman

THORNDIKE PRESS
A part of Gale, Cengage Learning

GALE
CENGAGE Learning

Farmington Hills, Mich • San Francisco • New York • Waterville, Maine
Meriden, Conn • Mason, Ohio • Chicago

This is a work of fiction. All of the characters, organizations, and events portrayed in this novel are either products of the author's imagination or are used fictitiously.

Thorndike Press® Large Print Mystery.
The text of this Large Print edition is unabridged.
Other aspects of the book may vary from the original edition.
Set in 16 pt. Plantin.

LIBRARY OF CONGRESS CATALOGING-IN-PUBLICATION DATA

Estleman, Loren D.
You know who killed me : an Amos Walker novel / by Loren D. Estleman.
— Large print edition.
pages cm. — (Thorndike Press large print mystery)
ISBN 978-1-4104-7700-2 (hardcover) — ISBN 1-4104-7700-2 (hardcover)
1. Walker, Amos (Fictitious character)—Fiction. 2. Private investigators—Fiction. 3. Large type books. I. Title.
PS3555.S84Y68 2015
813'.54—dc23 2014048943

Published in 2015 by arrangement with Tom Doherty Associates, LLC

Printed in Mexico
1 2 3 4 5 6 7 19 18 17 16 15

To Elmore Leonard (1925–2013).
Thanks, Dutch.

One

"Mister? I've got a confession to make."

"Yeah? Try a priest."

"I'm not a Catholic."

"Then find a cop."

I leaned along the bar and whispered in his ear: "I shot a man in Reno just to watch him die."

"You and Johnny Cash." He leaned the other direction, closing his hands around his glass.

"Reno's in Nevada."

"Last time I checked."

"What I can't figure out is why they put me in a California penal institution."

"You're drunk, pal."

"A non sequitur. I asked a simple question and I want a complicated answer."

He looked at me directly for the first time. He had a big face, red as a brick, a forehead stacked with wrinkles, and foreman written all over him. The saloon was a bare-bones affair across from the GM assembly plant in Highland Park; you didn't patronize it so much as wander inside because it stood between you and home. There was no pool table, no juke, and the toilet paper rolls in the men's room were padlocked. The bartender worked his way one direction with a pitcher of beer and the other with a bottle of Ten High. The job never ended. It was like painting the Big Mac bridge.

"Buddy, you don't stop breathing in my face, you'll get your answer."

"Show me your face and I'll breathe in it. I'm sick of looking at your butt."

He swung at me, but the joke was on him. I slid off the stool, but I never got as far as the floor. An angel dressed all in black folded her wings around me and bore me away from there.

They were pretty rough on me in rehab, but then they had to be: I was as hard as a hangnail and tough as suet. When after three weeks I was well enough to get dressed, I found a cigarette burn on my pants. Probably it had been there some time.

The physician who wound up in charge of my case was a tough little blonde with freckles, who spent most of the consultation in her office looking at my file on an Etch A

Sketch in her hand.

"You're lucky to be alive, you know."

"I know. I should take this streak to Vegas."

"You OD'd on alcohol and prescription drugs. We pumped enough Vicodin out of your stomach to put down King Kong. You've got the constitution of an ox, I'll say that. It says here you favor your left leg."

"Actually, I'm disappointed in it."

"Arthritis?"

"Thirty-ought-six."

"Which explains the scar on that thigh. There are others. A nasty one on your side, too high for an appendectomy. I think your skull was fractured once."

"Only once? I want a second opinion."

"What do you do for a living?"

"I'm a private eye."

"Fine, don't tell me. How are you feeling?"

"I could use a smoke."

"Is that supposed to be funny?"

"Am I laughing?"

"Mr. Walker, you were brought here instead of to jail, where you would've been booked for possession of a controlled substance without a valid prescription. The one you had expired years ago. You should have stopped taking Vicodin then, and you never should have drunk alcohol while you were taking it."

"I quit the pills over a year ago. I took them up again after I got into a foot chase that turned into the New York Marathon. I guess you could say I went into a tailspin after that."

"You were already in it. Look, I can approve your release, recommend you remain with us a while longer, or let the police do what the police do when someone breaks the law. It so happens we need your bed for someone who really wants to get better, and the jails are full of honest criminals, so I'll ask for assurance you'll seek professional help outside this institution to relieve you of your addiction. Yes?"

"On one condition."

"What's that?" She flicked a varnished fingernail at the screen she was holding.

"You make eye contact with me just once."

She looked up from her gizmo.

"Blue," I said. "Just as I thought."

There'd been more to it than simple pain, of course. I'd passed a milestone birthday I thought I'd never see — I hadn't expected to die before it, just had never seen myself being that age — and the only other one to acknowledge it was the place that services my Cutlass, along with a reminder that I was due for an oil change. Right on top of that I took a job looking for a lost child that had ended in the basement of a registered sex offender. The girl would have been about the age of my grandchild, if my marriage had stuck. I told the first cop on the scene the homeowner fell up a flight of stairs. The blue-collar bar they'd shoveled me out of a week later was just down the street from the kid who ordered my pills from Canada by way of the Internet.

I thought of celebrating my coming-out with a meal, but the smell of the restaurant when I stepped in the door stuck a lever under my stomach and turned it over. I went to Twelve Oaks Mall instead and got fitted for a new suit.

The tailor, a good-looking young black man in starched cuffs and collar, draped his tape measure back around his neck. "Forty-two long."

"I take a forty-four."

He measured again; an accommodating type. "Forty-two."

"It's always been forty-four."

He smiled.

" 'Always' isn't a word we use in my work. People gain weight and lose it. Have you been ill?"

"In a manner of speaking."

He rang up the sale. "We'll have the alterations done by the end of the week."

"By then it won't fit me. Where's the best place to eat around here?"

I was recovering, although not nearly as fast as I'd unrecovered.

I went to my office first. Rosecranz, the antediluvian super, was snapping new letters into the directory in the lobby. I read what he'd finished:

KARAOKE PR

"Public relations?"

"Press."

"Publisher?"

"I guess. The rest is 'E BOOKS.' "

"What's an e-book?"

"My great-grandniece has one. It's like a cell phone, only you read books on it. My day, you didn't need batteries to read."

"Those stone tablets are hard to lug around."

My olfactory sense had corrected itself. The two flights of stairs were haunted by the ghosts of nickel cigars, Black Jack gum, and forty rounds in the ring at the Kronk Boxing Club. A puff of stale air came out of my waiting room when I opened the door.

I'd left it unlocked for the inconvenience of clients. That had been a month ago.

The rock-hard bench and chipped coffee table were still there, also the magazines with Leon Spinks and Molly Ringwald on the covers. I unlocked the door to the sacristy, scooped up the pile of mail under the slot, dumped it on the desk, and opened the window on raw February. Detroit was far behind on snow that season. All the sins of summer and fall lay exposed on the dead grass and the streets had the cruel gray polished look of a printer's stone. The trees the county jail inmates had planted to dress up the place looked like twists of wire. A miniature foil top hat left over from New Year's Eve was stuck on a branch.

I'd missed the party, also a presidential inauguration and Groundhog Day, but there was still St. Valentine's to get through. I should have taken the doctor up on her offer and gone to the clink.

The ceiling fixture dimmed, then brightened. Karaoke Press had opened for business, overloading the building's Taft-era wiring. If the economy got any better, the corporation that owned the joint would have to remodel.

I dialed my voice-mail number and put it on speaker while I sorted mail. Someone wanted to sell me a long-term mortgage that would be paid off by my ghost; the owner of a gravel voice wanted me to kidnap his neighbor's barking dog; an online detective school invited me to serve on its faculty, my commission to be based on how many students I attracted; a woman who lengthened her vowels like a native Canadian wondered if I'd consider taking my fee in Dominion currency; General Motors had issued a recall on a car I hadn't owned in ten years; Gravel Voice said, look, if I didn't want to risk kidnapping the dog, I could just shoot it; my high school reunion was coming up again, just like quack grass; a man who whispered wanted me to search his geriatric nurse's apartment for his watch, wallet, and upper plate; a postcard signed by somebody I never heard of had an arrow pointing to his room in a hotel in Belize; Gravel Voice said to hell with it, he'd shoot the mutt himself. I lifted one foot off my desk and positioned the heel to break the connection.

"Walker, this is Ray Henty. I know how you feel about Iroquois Heights, but I wonder if you can come up and give me a hand."

The robotic voice belonging to the telephone company told me the call had come in just that morning. I dumped the mail, cut off the rest of my messages, and called the number of the police department that had given me more trouble than all the others combined.

"Lieutenant," I said, when I got Henty's extension. "Or is it captain now?"

"I'm lucky it isn't deputy, with a beat out in *Deliverance* country. You sound rough. Got a bug?"

"No. Just a monkey on my back. What's so important I have to go up there and get my head mailed back to me?"

"You know that's all changed since they gave the police department the boot. We're still chucking out the rotten eggs, but if anybody gives you grief, I'll have him up on charges so fast his pants will be down around his ankles."

"I've heard that before. You know how you can tell an egg's rotten? It always comes floating back to the top."

"Look, if you're afraid —"

"I'm afraid. I've only got one more concussion coming and I'm saving it for a woman in Eastpointe who works under the professional name Madame Mayhem."

"Okay. Jesus. As it so happens, this isn't something I want to talk about in the Heights. Will you come to my house? It's outside trigger-happy pistol range."

"What's up?"

"You know who killed me. That's what's up."

Two

Ray Henty lived in a bedroom community as old as Iroquois Heights; at some point in the era of whistle-stop campaigns, it had taken itself out of the running for county seat, and dodged the stink of suburban politics. There was a hardware store downtown that sold nails by the pound and old-growth oaks flanked the residential streets. A brew pub had opened in the old neighborhood movie theater since the last time I drove through. That would have made the front page if the place still had a newspaper.

Yet another mayor of the Heights was under federal indictment, and a petition to dissolve the police department had put the issue up to the voters. This time, even the disappearance of three ballot boxes had failed to maintain the status quo. The county sheriff's department set up a substation in the old city hall, with Lieutenant Henty in command. The situation was desperate enough to waive the ordinance requiring residency inside the city limits.

He'd earned the appointment. I'd worked with him a couple of times when he headed the Missing Persons division at headquarters; for a cop he was friendly to a plastic badge, and he had a talent for getting various branches of law enforcement to cooperate. He'd never once fired his sidearm except to qualify, which working that close to Detroit said something about his ability to contain a situation.

Henty didn't waste time. Before he sat down at his new desk, he brought in an outside firm to recalibrate the parking meters so that they didn't shave five minutes off every hour and sent deputies to confiscate the gadgets that changed all the red lights to green for cars driven by wives of petty city officials. Of course he made enemies: Someone dug up a former suspect in a chain of burglaries who said Deputy Henty had ruptured his eardrum during an interrogation fifteen years ago, a female corrections officer in the county jail announced that he'd made unwelcome sexual advances to her when he was a sergeant. They later recanted, and a former member of the local police commission was charged with suborning to commit perjury.

Soon he had company. Henty personally swung a sledge against a wall in the old police evidence room and found the priest-hole containing all the cash and confiscated heroin that had vanished from inventory due to an error in accounting. That had led to more indictments, an extradition from Uruguay, and an invitation to the lieutenant to speak at a national criminologists' convention in Las Vegas.

Which he declined. "Too busy." Translation: "I don't want to walk into my suite and find a hooker waiting for me with her press agent."

The house was a small brick mansard with a fake widow's walk on the roof and a brick carriage house in back. He called to me from there after I slammed my door in the driveway. Dusk was drifting in; yellow light framed him where he stood holding open one of the double doors.

"Where's Mister Ed?" I sank my paw deep in his, sparing my fingers.

He gave me his iron grin. He was a U.S. Marine vet and looked the part, jarhead and all, in an old white dress shirt rolled up past his biceps, corduroys, and scuffed sneakers. He was fifty, but could pass for midthirties in the right light. "You look like shit. You ought to give up red meat."

"Also booze, cigarettes, painkillers, and all other forms of entertainment. I hit into the rough. I'm all right now."

"Keep telling yourself that. Maybe you'll buy it. Show you something." He stepped aside to let me come in, closed the door behind me, and made sure of it with a hook-and-eye. Then he took three steps and snatched the blue tarp off a white 1966 Ford Fairlane with red vinyl seats, russet in patches where the primer had worn through.

"Is that what I think it is?"

"See for yourself." He jerked his square chin toward the hood.

I rapped on it, got a dull thud.

"Yep. Fiberglass cold-air hood. Only fifty-seven ever built. Soon as I find a trans, I'll match it to that piece-of-crap Cutlass of yours mile for mile."

"Don't underestimate that piece of crap. I keep all the dirt and rust on the outside for show. They're going to say you grafted to get this."

"That's why I keep receipts, and have myself audited every year. If they want me off the job they'd better use a gun. Don't tell Vicky I said that. She's superstitious."

"Then don't say it." I looked around. He'd lined the place with pegboard and hung it with stainless steel tools: bling for the gearhead. An electric chain fall perched in a cross-timber above the car and he had a roll of industrial transparent plastic stored in the rafters, to seal off the vehicle when it came time to spray paint. A redhead gripped a welding torch in a picture on a calendar on the wall, wearing knee-high boots and a welder's helmet with the visor tipped up, nothing else.

"You could bottle the air in here and sell testosterone."

He replaced the tarp, rolling it carefully from rear bumper to front: so much for small talk. I took out a pack of cigarettes, raising my eyebrows.

"Go ahead," he said. "Burn yourself down from the inside. Just don't touch off the gas tank."

"Thanks. I was afraid I'd get a lecture." I lit up and blew a plume of smoke at Miss February. "What did you mean, 'You know who killed me'?"

"Where you been since the beginning of the year, under a rock?"

"Yeah."

"Christ, I wish you had company."

He led me outside and pointed his chin at a tall floodlit billboard a hundred yards away from where we were standing, faced away from us at a slight angle. It had a giant blow-up photograph of a smiling middle-aged man under a legend six feet tall:

"YOU KNOW WHO KILLED ME!"

At the bottom, in letters and numerals nearly as large, was the tip line for the sheriff's department.

The man was wearing a cable-knit sweater embroidered with reindeer.

We went back inside. The heat from the oil stove in the corner felt good after the dank cold.

"Taken over Christmas. They don't come much fresher. That sign faces the expressway. There are four more just like it, scattered around like Easter eggs, only a damn sight more visible. Paid for by the widow."

"Who is he?"

"Donald Gates. Thirty-eight. We scraped him out of his basement New Year's Day, shot twice in the head."

"Drug killing?"

"If he was pushing, he was craftier than any dealer I ever heard of. No sign of drugs on the premises, nothing showed up at the autopsy. I had to bet? No. No out-of-the-ordinary deposits or withdrawals in his banking records, no history of gambling.

The only one he owed money to was his mortgage lender, and he was on top of his payments. Anyway Fifth Third isn't employing strong-arms this year."

"What's the status?"

"We're following up on some promising leads."

"I'm not a reporter, Lieutenant."

"Okay. We're tapped out. Average Joe, by all accounts: not rich, not important, stay-at-home wife, one-point-five kids, a few friends, fewer enemies, and they're all accounted for. Robbery's out; wife found nothing missing."

"Where'd he work?"

"City of Iroquois Heights. Maintained the computer that operates the traffic lights."

"Maybe somebody got stuck at a red and took it out on him."

"I've heard stupider reasons. The last person to see him was the guard in the building where they keep the mainframe. He told his fellow workers he was going home to change, then join his wife at some friends' New Year's Eve party. When he didn't show and didn't answer his cell or the phone at home, she went there and found him in the rec room in the basement. Two nine-millimeter slugs behind the right ear." He pointed a finger at the spot behind his and waggled his thumb twice.

"And I come into this how?"

He leaned back against his workbench, crossing his arms. "Legwork. His wife thinks we're dragging our feet, hoping the case will go away; that's why the billboards. She's thinking of the wrong cops, but I guess I can't blame her for that based on past history. Gates's life insurance is footing the bill probably. The local press picked it up and put it out on the wire. It's national now."

"No surprise. It's a catchy line."

"Yeah. So now we're getting calls from all over the country on top of the tips we always get locally, on *top* of all the routine meshuga that goes with a homicide investigation. They all have to be run down, and I've only got fifteen deputies to do the running."

I crushed out my cigarette on the concrete floor. "I don't like where this is going."

"Maybe you've got something better to do."

"Maybe you know more about what rock I've been under than you made out."

"My old partner is deputy chief in Highland Park. He made the call to stick you in rehab instead of the county lockup. We go out for a beer now and then. Listen, if you're not up to it —"

"Leave that reverse-psyche stuff to the shrinks. What can I do that fifteen men good and true can't?"

"It isn't that they can't. I need people to answer the phones and sift through the evidence and stay on top of the state cops to report on DNA before another New Year's rolls around, and refill the coffeemaker." He straightened up, opened a drawer in a rolling toolbox, and took out a green file folder stamped PROPERTY I.H.P.D.; the new management hadn't had time to change the name on all the stationery.

I took the folder, flipped it open, and looked at three pages of telephone numbers.

"You want me to run down *all* the tips?"

"The U.S. Army couldn't run them all down by summer. Those are just the ones that came without names."

"Anonymous tips come with phone numbers?"

"Thanks to caller ID. Don't let it get around. If people find out it's all Kris Kringle and Peter Cottontail, they'll stop calling. Once in a couple of hundred times it pays off."

"This is where I ask what's in it for me."

"A deputy's salary. And something you've never had before: the good will of the authorities in Iroquois Heights."

I riffled the rest of the papers in the folder. There were at least thirty pages, including a copy of the original complaint, information based on notes taken by the responding deputies, and progress reports.

I snapped it shut. “Nosy neighbors, gossip addicts, cranks, pranksters, axe-grinders, attention hounds, and fruitcakes. Thanks for the job, Lieutenant.”

“Throw fortune hunters into the mix. The church the Gateses attended is offering ten thousand dollars for information leading to a conviction.”

“I knew something was missing.”

“Now raise your right hand.”

I looked, but there was no sign of humor on the chiseled face. “I hope we’re getting ready to say the pledge of allegiance.”

“No such luck. I can’t justify paying department wages to a private op. It’s against regulations to give those reports to a civilian. It’s still dicey this way, but swearing you in gives me something to say in my defense at the hearing. I’m not issuing you a shield, and that honorary star you break the law with every time you flash it belongs to the wrong county. Leave it home.”

I wondered how he knew about that.

“Do I get a whistle?”

“Just raise your right hand.”

When that was done, he opened another drawer and gave me a portable tape player. "It's a two-hour tape. The calls were recorded in the order the numbers are listed. There's a sheet with names and addresses in the folder, taken from a reverse directory. Which ones you follow up on is up to you. The comedians and nutcases generally give themselves away, but not always; which is why I decided to put a trained detective on this detail. The ones I have are too busy pulling Gates's life apart and putting it back together.

"I'm only giving you the details of the case so you can separate the wheat from the chaff. Don't interview any other witnesses, stay away from the wife, and don't tell anyone you're a deputy. My neck's stuck out far enough as it is."

"What do I tell the callers when they ask where I got their number?"

He smiled. "That's why I gave the job to an outsider. You're going to take the flack for crooking the system. When it gets out a private snooper found his way into our files, I'll call a press conference to express official outrage."

"They can use you in Washington."

"One more thing. If you put this job on your résumé and anyone checks, you lied."

"This just keeps getting better and better."

He stopped smiling. "I can't turn it down, but you can. Nobody'd blame you."

I stuck the folder under my arm. "It's either this or a gig at the Eureka Cyber School of Criminal Science."

"Thanks, Amos."

Both my arms were occupied, so I got away from there without any more pulverized bones in my fingers.

Outside, I turned my collar up against the cold. Donald Gates smiled at me. It was one of those pictures that follow you around.

Three

I smoked half a pack in my easy chair, listening to the voices on the tape player, checking off numbers to follow up on and drawing lines through the rejects. There weren't nearly enough of the last. At midnight I switched off the machine, went to bed, and dreamed I lived in a cubicle, trying to sell storm doors to whoever answered the telephone.

Operator: *Sheriff's tip line. What's your information?*

Caller: *Yeah. I know who killed Donald Gates.*

Operator: *I'm listening.*

Caller: *Not over the phone. How do I know you won't just nab the guy and stiff me on the reward?*

Operator: *Sir, that reward is being offered by Christ Church, not by this department.*

Caller: *Okay, forget it. I'll call the church.*

Operator: *If you're certain of your information, withholding it from the authorities is a crime.*

Caller: *You'll get it after I talk to the church.*

He'd hung up then. He had a deep voice with a hint of a twang. I looked up his name on the sheet taken from the reverse directory: Alvinus C. Adams, 1207 Daniel Boone Drive, Iroquois Heights; a lot of streets got their names from people who fought the Indians the town was named for. It put him a couple of blocks over from the Gateses, a hopeful sign. I finished my morning coffee and dialed the number.

"Hello?" The same voice.

"Mr. Adams? My name is Amos Walker. I'm a private detective."

"No shit? I thought they went out with black-and-white TV."

"Not just yet. You called the sheriff's tip line two weeks ago, claiming to know who killed Donald Gates."

"Where the hell'd you get that?" he said after a silence. "It's supposed to be anonymous."

I'd lain awake much of the night working on an explanation. I'd decided just to duck it.

"How far did you get with Christ

Church?"

"What's it to you?"

"I'm guessing from your attitude you didn't get far."

"I didn't get dick, same as from the law. Why do they set up tip lines and offer *re*wards if they don't want the help?"

"If your information's good, I might be able to help you get half that reward."

"Who gets the other half, as if I don't know the answer already?"

I grinned at the empty seat opposite me in the breakfast nook.

"Mr. Adams, that's the most pointless question I've ever been asked. Did you mean what you said about Gates's murderer?"

"I'll axe you the same question I axed the bitch at the sheriff's. What's to keep you from taking what I give you and keeping the whole thing for yourself?"

"Have you got a pencil?"

"Sure I got a pencil. I just ain't got a job. That's why I'm going against ten generations of Adamses and turning stool pigeon. What am I writing?"

I gave him the names and numbers of three references, one of them a congressman who'd served his Michigan district more than thirty years. "Ask them the same thing you asked me. You can believe them or not, but there will be a record you asked, which would make it difficult for me to snipe you out of what you've got coming."

"What's your name again?"

I repeated it.

"Then again, you could be somebody else saying you're Walker, and nobody'll ever know who took that money."

"You just screw yourself into bed every night, don't you?"

"I wasn't born this way, pal."

"They'd know at Christ Church who took the money. But after you make those calls — and the numbers are easy enough to check, in case you think they belong to accomplices — we'll meet, and I'll show you my bona fides. What've you got to lose?"

"Not my job, that's for sure." He took my numbers, home, office, cell, and the call was over.

I tried three more numbers from the record, got a recording, no answer, and a harried-sounding woman with children slaughtering each other in the background who told me her husband wouldn't be home till six. I thanked her and said I'd call then. I didn't leave my name or any message.

I opened the folder again. Christ Episcopal

Church, the Gateses' place of worship, had stood near downtown Detroit since 1863. Its current pastor was Florence Melville.

My ear was sore from holding the receiver against it. A little face-to-face spirituality is never a bad idea.

When I put the cordless phone back in its cradle in the living room, the card the tough little blond doctor had given me poked out from under the standard. It belonged to a private therapist in Redford Township; but it wasn't the time to make good on the deal.

The Cutlass's cold engine turned over twice and caught. On the way to the river I saw another "YOU KNOW WHO KILLED ME!" billboard, Donald Gates smiling in his festive sweater. I might have seen it before, but only through a cloud that still hadn't quite passed.

The sign didn't mention the reward, but it was the widow behind the advertising, not the church.

I peeled the cigarette I'd just lit from my lip, wound the window down two inches, and poked it into the slipstream. It had all the flavor of a toothpick. My belly ached and the "Jingle Bells" dogs were barking in my head. You know you're going to survive when you least feel like it.

I paralleled the chalk-gray water until I

got to Rivard and swung into the parking lot next to the old pile.

The churches are almost all that's left from the days before Henry Ford, and there isn't much left from those days either. The city is North America's leading manufacturer of vacant lots. Christ Episcopal has loads of spiked railings for pigeons to curl their toes around and a belfry screaming for bats and plenty of them. It's probably haunted. All the self-respecting spirits have moved out of city hall.

There was no service in progress. In the echoing nave, a novice or whatever he was stopped pushing his carpet sweeper to direct me to the rectory. I went that way, smelling candle wax, furniture oil, and dust. I'd been raised Episcopalian, but had drifted. It was the first time in many years I felt the urge to genuflect. I resisted; the saints in the alcoves were watching, and they didn't get there by being gullible. The non-martyrs, anyway.

I needed a battering ram to make sure my knock would be heard on the other side of the rectory door, but after a second a voice called out for me to enter. The door swung open easily on a system of counterweights or something and I eased it shut behind me. The ceiling was high enough to vanish beyond reach of the sunlight coming through the leaded-glass window. Gray as it was, the light was still bright enough to blur the figure sitting at a desk in front of it.

The desk itself resembled a beached Spanish galleon, all beveled panels and carved laurels, with a red leather top. There was plenty of red in that room, in the deep rug framed all around by eight inches of polished floor, in a dim gilt-bordered painting of some bloody biblical battle leaning out from the wall on guy wires, and in a bronze pen stand studded with garnets on the near edge of the desk. Red's the boss color in the spectrum of the faith. It took me back to the red front door on St. Erasmus, a long time ago.

Erasmus: put to death, they said, by having his intestines unwound from his body by a windlass. I'd let go of just about everything else I'd learned there, but I wasn't about to forget that.

"Yes?" The woman behind the desk looked up from her writing.

"Reverend Melville?"

"Yes," she said. "*That* Melville, in answer to your next question. Unfortunately the copyright on *Moby Dick* ran out a hundred years before I was born."

Close up, she was a sturdy brunette with

a heart-shaped face and gray eyes behind gold-framed glasses. She wore a white silk blouse with a ruffle and a touch of gloss on her lips; it was a progressive parish, for all its antiquity. A streak of silver started at her hairline to the right of the center part, spreading whisk broom–like for three inches. She wasn't decrepit; I figured her for early thirties. An old church superstition said that when the Call was genuine, it left just such a mark.

Florence Melville smiled. She'd caught the path of my gaze.

"Yes," she said again. "Started, no doubt, by a clergyman with the same streak. It's a birthmark. It goes as far as the scalp, as I found out when I hit my head on a swing when I was nine and they shaved it to patch me up. Back then I was going to be a country singer."

"I wanted to be Robert Mitchum."

"You came close."

"Don't go by these eyelids. I haven't been sleeping a lot."

"Is that what you came to talk about?"

You can spend all day making up your mind or letting it make up itself. I spilled the beans.

"My name's Walker, ma'am. I'm a private detective, working with the sheriff's lieutenant in Iroquois Heights on the Gates murder." I showed her my ID. "I'd appreciate it if that didn't leave this room. Some of the people I might have to ask questions open up easier when they think they're talking to a free agent."

Her smile went away and a crease of pain split the skin between her eyebrows. "Sit down, please, Mr. Walker."

I hauled a walnut chair formerly used as a throne by Charlemagne up to the desk and sat. It felt more comfortable than it looked.

The Reverend Melville folded her hands on the yellow pad she'd been scribbling on. "I've met Lieutenant Henty. My guess is he's in favor of keeping your secret."

"He's a good cop. Unfortunately, he works for a public servant, whose opponents in the next election would say he couldn't do his job without outside help. It's hogwash, but the voters love to watch politicians mud wrestle. Anyway you don't strike me as someone I can string along with a fish story, and I seem to remember something about priests being good at keeping secrets."

"Most priests, yes. I can't name exceptions without becoming one myself. The Gateses were beloved of this congregation. Whenever volunteers were needed, they were in front of the line. Amelie made items for the bake sale and Don donated a thousand dollars toward the new roof three years ago. Both sold candy bars in front of Wal-Mart to support Youth Camp. To go on would be redundant. Can you tell me anything you've learned about this vile crime?"

"Sorry, no. I just started, and in theory I'm not working the case except to run down some anonymous phone tips. That way those involved with the actual investigation can concentrate on that instead of —"

"Trivia." She sat back, deflated.

"I was going to say 'the minutiae.' There wouldn't be a tip line if concerned citizens didn't shed light sometimes."

"It helps if there's profit in it. I'm sure you know about the reward. It was offered by a loyal parishioner who doesn't want publicity."

"Then he should button up his pocketbook. Mixing money into a police investigation is like throwing honey on an anthill."

"May I ask why you're here, if you're not really investigating? I'm not one of your anonymous callers."

I almost said, "I know"; but you can load someone with only so many secrets before she collapses. "Professional hazard. You can't just nibble at a potato chip."

"How can I help?"

"For starters, I'd like to talk to whoever put up that reward."

"Impossible, for the reason I already gave you. Why? Are you that desperate for suspects?"

"The problem with not having any is it makes everyone suspicious. If this party is as loyal to the church as you say, it might be a way of assuaging his or her guilt. On the other hand, it could be a heavy-handed way of diverting suspicion from himself. Herself?"

She didn't rise to that bait. "I can believe the first, although not of this particular person. The second; well, that only works in movies, doesn't it? And not even then."

"Yeah. The police don't divert so easy. I'd hate to be a close-up magician at a cop convention. All our guilty benefactor would do is call attention away from everyone else. I'd like to talk to him — her — whoever — anyway. If he cares that much, it means he knew the Gateses well. Maybe better than anyone. Disregarding a random killing — and the execution style says this one was personal — the closer I can get to the victim, the closer I can get to the perpetrator."

"Lieutenant Henty made that same argument. My answer was the same. He didn't like it. He said there's a gray area when it comes to privileged communication — did this offer come out during confession, is it part of confession, or can it be interpreted as a conversation involving two people rather than a priest and a penitent? I wouldn't give him even that much. I like it here. How long do you think I'd remain in this assignment once it was learned I betrayed one of the flock?"

I met her gray eyes, hard as polar caps and as cold. "Cops keep secrets too."

"From their wives, maybe. They're rarely forced to submit written reports at home, and that's one place reporters can't make a stink out of being denied access to what's supposed to be public record. Then, too, Henty works for a politician, as you said. That kind leaks from every orifice."

"Yuck. Okay, that's dropped. How well did you know Gates?"

She glanced down at the sermon she was writing, or maybe it was a shopping list. Whatever she was looking for there, she found it. She looked at me.

"Nearly as well as Amelie. Don and I dated."

Four

"When?"

She lifted a pair of strong eyebrows. "You're not shocked?"

"I've probably heard as many confessions as you, Reverend."

"At the risk of disappointing you, there was nothing scandalous about it. It was ten years ago, before I was ordained, and before he met Amelie. We grew up in the same neighborhood, in Monroe; not that we knew each other very well then. We met again here when I was attending divinity school and he was installing the traffic computer in Iroquois Heights.

"We didn't have sex," she said. "I'm not saying we wouldn't have; priesthood in my faith doesn't come with a chastity clause, although premarital relations while I was studying Scripture might have been a stumbling block. I wasn't a virgin. But we figured out fairly early we were meant to be friends, not lovers."

I hadn't asked. People who respected other people's confidences seldom needed encouragement to talk about themselves.

"What was he like?"

"You mean, without the hazy gloss of death? A nice fellow, but a bit dull. He talked a lot about computers. Sharing his last name with Bill Gates may have had something to do with his career choice. Offhand I'd say the only color in his life was his annual fishing trip to Quebec. That's where he met his wife, after we stopped pretending we had anything in common. She's French-Canadian."

"That explains her name. Did they get along?"

She picked up the pen she'd been writing with and put it back down, squared with the edge of the yellow pad. "Once again, you're skating close to my oath. I will say they didn't have any serious problems. Certainly not enough for Amelie to commit murder."

"I wouldn't say certainly. Everyone else's problems look simple compared to ours. Wives have been known to kill their husbands over a toilet lid. But I wasn't suggesting that. I'm just trying to get a picture."

"Good people, both of them. Normal

child, full of boy-juice. Maybe a little too much, but that's between him and his pediatrician. Amelie was three months pregnant when it happened. She miscarried."

"I'm sorry."

"I think you are," she said after a moment. "They say God never gives you more than you can handle. I sometimes wonder. But she's determined to bring the one responsible to justice. The billboard was her idea." She frowned. "That's the phrase, isn't it? 'Bring to justice'?"

"The Old Testament was plenty clear on the definition of the term."

"So was the New. I'm often called on to referee."

"When's the last time you saw Gates?"

"Christmas morning, when the family attended services. I spoke to them briefly afterward."

"How'd he seem?"

"How does anyone seem on that occasion? They're generally on their best behavior."

"Nothing unusual."

"Not that I noticed, but it was only a couple of minutes. It was standing room only; some people think He keeps a list, like Santa. I had a lot of hands to shake at the door on the way out." She rolled the pen up to the edge of the pad. "What's your experience with this kind of investigation?"

"More than I liked at the time. My Yellow Pages ad says I specialize in missing persons. Some are more missing than others."

"I suppose you have references."

"Isn't it a little late for that, after answering all these questions?"

"Not if it turns out you're worth hiring to find Don Gates's killer."

"I've got a job," I said after a moment. "It's the same case. There'd be a conflict."

"It's the same case, but a different job. Henty's got you running errands. I'm considering asking you to solve it."

"That's a thin line."

"How old are you, Mr. Walker?"

"I'm no longer middle-aged."

"Offhand I'd say you put on a few extra years recently. Your collar's loose, and you don't strike me as a man who's careless in his dress. You've been sick."

"This isn't confession, Reverend."

"Sorry. I digressed. My point was you're old enough to have been doing what you do for a long time. I'd say you're no stranger to a thin line."

Just for fun I gave her some names and numbers; not the same as I'd given Alvinus

Adams of Daniel Boone Drive. You can lose valuable contacts snagging up their time with phone calls.

I excused myself while she was dialing and went outside for a smoke. A few yards above my head a gash had opened in the overcast, spilling watery sunlight and no heat. Out on the river, the tug that delivered the mail to passing ore carriers slid up one side of a steely wave, balanced for a moment on the point, then slid down the other side. The service wasn't necessary; the post office went along with it for the sake of local color. The way things were going it would be discontinued quicker than Saturday delivery.

It was snowing on the Windsor side, flakes as big as Canadian quarters. It made our side look even bleaker than always. One of those drenching springs was coming, the ones that raise the levels of the Great Lakes and the hopes of governors who want to sell water to Arizona.

The Reverend Florence Melville was cradling the receiver when I let myself back into the rectory. I sat down in the Charlemagne chair and crossed my legs.

"You're not running for Man of the Year, are you?" She looked like she'd been having a good time.

"You asked for references. The people who like me aren't in a position to impress you."

"The consensus seems to be you make more trouble for yourself than you have to, and it's contagious."

"Not to clients."

"They're agreed on that too. What annoys them most is what I found most impressive. You don't carry tales, even when it would free you up to do your job."

"Not carrying tales *is* the job. You said the same thing about yours."

"While you were out polluting the atmosphere, did you reach any conclusions about whether my offer represents a conflict of interest?"

"It's a thin line, like I said. I'd be bending it, but I've done that before. It hasn't broken yet."

"What do you charge?"

"Five hundred a day; three days up front, for expenses."

"As much as that?"

"I never know when I might have to catch a plane in a hurry. You get back what I don't spend if the job runs shorter, minus my labor. I wouldn't count on it this time. Even when there's an army of cops, the average murder investigation runs several weeks when the culprit isn't actually caught red-handed; that's a conservative estimate since Detroit closed its police lab. They just found some rape kits they overlooked for twenty years."

"Are you at all tempted by the reward?"

"Not without knowing who put it up. I can't remember the last time one was paid. It always gets spent somehow, and the bookkeeping always checks. Then there's the chance the money man's the one responsible for the crime, in which case I'd never see a cent due to my own damn brilliance. The interests don't get more conflicted than that." I brushed the telltale ash off my suitcoat. "What's your end, apart from having lost a valuable parishioner?"

"Donald Gates was also my friend. So is Amelie. In my work they don't come by the bushel. Friendship means letting your hair down, and no one wants to fart in the presence of a priest. Call it pride, but I can't let a personal injury like this pass. Don't remind me what the Lord said about vengeance; I'm the referee, remember?"

"Will the Church go along with it?"

"It won't have to. I'm paying you out of my own pocket."

I watched her open a drawer and take out a checkbook bound in red vinyl. She picked up her pen.

"I'd have to insist you put all other cases aside," she said, writing; "with the exception, of course, of your obligation to the sheriff's department. Running down anonymous tips would be part of the deal anyway."

I grinned. "Just don't tell Henty. I'd like to get used to coming and going in the Heights without getting rabbit-punched or thrown in the hoosegow."

Five

Operator: *Sheriff's tip line. What's your information?*

Caller: *You need to check out Donald Gates's fellow workers at city.*

Operator: *Which ones, ma'am?*

Caller: *Not until I see the money.*

Operator: *If you leave your name, I'll have an officer get in touch with you.*

Caller: *The billboard said I don't have to give my name.*

Operator: *Without a name, the church can't make out the check.*

Caller: *What's wrong with "cash"?*

Operator: *Would you like to speak to an officer?*

Caller: *Let me think about it.*

The caller's voice was female, no accent except maybe Midwestern. Her name was Carol Thompson. She was a neighbor of Ray Henty's, ten blocks removed, on the other side of the boulevard that separated the little town from Iroquois Heights. Another possibility.

This time I didn't call. I had the cassette tape playing in the dashboard and only one bar showing on my Fisher-Price cell phone; a dropped call is the worst way to make a good first impression. I took the Chrysler Expressway from Jefferson and drove again through the quiet streets until I came to a ranch-style house with garage attached. Christmas lights were still attached to the roof, but they weren't burning by daylight, and maybe not at all until next December. Some people leave them up all year.

"Ms. Thompson?" I asked the woman who answered the door. She wore red-and-black buffalo plaid over a pink T-shirt with SUPER BITCH lettered across it in blue letters. Black tights encased legs ending in red knuckles and thick yellow nails sticking out of open-toed mules. She was shaped like a witch's cauldron inverted on top of a sawhorse. Her age was whatever you like.

"Mrs.," she snapped. "Please go away. I keep telling you people I'm a Christian. I don't witness."

"I'm not peddling *The Watchtower,* Mrs. Thompson." I showed her the ID. "I'm a Michigan State Police–licensed private investigator, looking into the Donald Gates homicide."

A dim glimmer of brainpower showed in a pair of mud-colored eyes; disregarding everything I'd said between "State Police" and "Donald Gates." It was all in the order of how you identified yourself. As the taxidermist said, I can give you an eagle or a duck using the same materials.

"I don't know what you're talking about."

"You indicated a coworker of Gates's is responsible for his death. I have to run all these reports down, Mrs. Thompson."

"But, how — ?"

"People gossip. May I come in? They're recalling the company car because of a faulty heater. I'm frozen through and through." A Big Wheel tricycle stood on the winter-killed grass of the lawn. I was counting on maternal instinct.

"Let me see that card again. Roy don't like me inviting in strangers."

I let her see it again. She lip-read it from top to bottom.

"Okay, I guess. But just the front room."

The doorway led straight into a living room with a pea-green shag rug, a console TV and stereo with a converter box plopped on top, a Christmas-tree lamp next to a brown plush recliner, and a jumble of splashy paperback novels and *Reader's Digests* on a coffee table made of faux-medieval dark wood and antiqued brass rivets. If the TV were on, Sonny and Cher could sass each other and nobody would think it odd. The house smelled of Twinkies deep-fried in hog fat.

"I don't have much time," she said. "I design Web sites, and people who want Web sites aren't patient people."

A door stood open on what should have been a spare bedroom, where a flat-screen monitor displayed a bunch of information that meant as much to me as sushi in Switzerland.

At her invitation I sat in the plush chair. It offered no resistance all the way down to the frame; I was already worrying about getting back up out of it. "I'll try not to take up too much of your time. What do you know about where Donald Gates worked?"

She lowered herself into an upholstered rocker printed all over with deer made from Legos; they made me think of the reindeer on Gates's Christmas sweater. Probably no connection. Michigan has more deer than it has lakes.

"What about the reward?" she asked.

"It's still there, accumulating interest. Waiting for someone to collect it."

"I want that in writing."

"You've already got it. Seen a billboard lately?" But just to be friendly I took out my wallet, dealt out a hundred in twenties, and stuck them under *Prom Midnight* on the coffee table. On the cover a pasty-faced teenage boy with fangs was noshing on the neck of a pubescent girl in the backseat of a Dodge Viper. "Consider it a down payment."

She didn't move; which is quite a feat when you're sitting in a rocking chair. "From here that don't look like one-tenth of ten percent of ten grand."

"Actually, that's just what it is. It's a gesture of good faith. If I like what I hear based on this conversation, it stays."

She rocked then, forward, back. "Just 'cause I was born in Idaho don't mean I tried to outstare a potato. I know what I know and it'll cost you to know the same."

I looked at a Thomas Kinkade print on the wall above the rocking chair: a mill wheel turning next to a gingerbread house. There are never any people in them.

"That's almost poetry, Mrs. Thompson. Withholding information in a felony is a felony. The law sees it as accessory after the fact. From the looks of this room, I'm pretty sure you're familiar with *Cops.* I'm offering you cash money as a surety against what's coming if we nail this bird. The other side of the coin is you go to jail."

The rocker stopped. It had never rocked at all; that had been an illusion.

"I get the hundred either way," she said. "You like, you don't like, you leave it behind."

I stretched out my leg and planted my heel on the book.

"I don't like, it goes with me. I like, you stay out of jail."

Her voice climbed to a whine. "How'd I get in this kind of trouble? I just made a phone call!"

I yawned, genuinely. I'd had one of those nights.

Pudgy fingers drummed an upholstered arm. "My husband's a maintenance man in the building where Gates worked. He heard another employee complaining about how cushy Gates's job was; sit around all day pushing buttons and looking at monitors."

"That's it?"

"I'm not finished. He said, 'Problem with being a civil servant is you can't get fired. Killing a guy's the only way to move up.' "

"What's the name?"

"It's foreign. It'll come to me."

I switched heels on the vampire's face and

watched her concentrate. It was like waiting for the mill wheel in the painting to move.

"Yako!" she barked. It sounded like a successful Heimlich. "Yuri Yako; I remembered the two *y*'s."

I got out my notebook. "That's y-u-r-i y-a-k-o?"

"How should I know? I never saw it written. What is it, Russian?"

"The Yuri part, anyway."

"Roy didn't say if he had an accent, but I guess he'd have to, wouldn't he, or he'd have changed his name to something American by now, just to get along."

"Maybe he's proud of his heritage. Irving Wallace's son changed his name back to Wallechinsky."

"I don't know who that is."

"Your husband's sure that's what he said, 'Killing a guy's the only way up'?"

"He's not likely to forget it. What about the hundred?"

I looked at what I'd written. After a moment I took my foot off the coffee table and stood up, leaving the money there.

I think it was the name that made up my mind, although I don't know why. Maybe it was the romantic in me. It helped take away the bitter taste of playing the bully.

■ ■ ■ ■

Driving away from there I got a call. The number on the screen belonged to Alvinus C. Adams.

"Okay, you check out," he said. "Where you want to meet?"

I said, "Let's make it convenient for you. Got a favorite hangout?" People open up better in familiar places. Also a place local to him put me closer to Yuri Yako.

"None I can afford, and I don't want you picking up the check and charging it against what I got coming. I got an interview in Detroit at four. I'll drop by your office after."

I looked at my watch. It was coming up on noon. I said okay and punched out.

The address I got for Iroquois Heights Traffic Control was an old school building in a residential neighborhood, three stories of brick and frame with one of those old-fashioned chutes I bet the kids had loved to slide down during fire drills, and 1931 chiseled in the cornerstone. The place had a truncated, out-of-proportion look, as if something was missing from the original construction, a bell tower or something gone to demolition. A sign in the parking lot read:

EMPLOYEES ONLY
ALL OTHERS WILL BE TOWED

I parked on the street and fed the meter. They said things were different now, but the changes might not have worked their way down to free enterprise. For as long as I could remember, violators were fair game for any independent with a winch on his truck; he split the fines with the city, and probably with whoever put through the paperwork.

Inside, the place smelled like cheap varnish and dry rot. The original teal-colored linoleum was worn through to the floorboards in craters, and the boards themselves were so warped that crossing them made you woozy, like walking down the aisle of a train car rocking on the rails. A freestanding sign with arrows directed visitors to where they could pay fines or obtain information.

A Plexiglas shield protected the woman at the Information counter from citizens. A circular metal grate had been inserted into it for communication. I wanted to ask for a ticket to the matinee.

She ran a fingernail down a clipboard

looking for Yuri Yako's name. She wore trifocals and a skyscraper wig someone had combed under LBJ; the marks would still be there when we got our first female president. "Three-twelve." The grate muffled her voice. "Third floor."

"Where else would you keep it?"

"What?"

I shook my head and went to the stairs. They passed between lath-and-plaster partitions with a green metal fire door at the bottom, propped open with an iron horse block. They squeaked, of course. I avoided gripping the brass railing with its generations of bacilli and spirilla. On the second flight I met a character coming down in a tweed three-piece suit and tortoiseshell glasses carrying a jumble of green cardboard file folders under one arm, papers sticking out from them at all angles. We both said "Pardon me," and passed each other sideways. I caught a whiff of Old Spice and Jack Daniel's.

On the top landing I paused to drag oxygen into a pair of lungs cured in smoke, then followed more worn linoleum under a series of milk-colored globe fixtures until I came to 312 at the end. It was paneled oak, layered with old varnish atop generations of grit, a craquelure effect, with a wire grid sandwiched between frosted glass panes. It was a corner office and in school days would probably have belonged to the principal, or some other administrator worthy of maximum security.

The door was unlocked. I let myself in.

The big double-hung windows of Depression-era commercial construction had given way to heat-saving panels. The linoleum had been replaced with dark blue static-free carpet and fluorescent tubes hung in troughs from the ceiling. The only noise came from an ionizer, whirring as it scrubbed dust and airborne spores from the atmosphere. The computer itself, a row of monitors set on a long painted particle-board table operated by a single keyboard, was silent. The man seated at it with his back to me slurped coffee from a white enamel mug without a clever slogan and set it down.

"Yuri Yako?"

He swiveled his ergonomic chair, showing no surprise; he'd probably seen my reflection in the glass of one of the monitors. He was about thirty, slender, with black hair cut close to the skull and small ears flush with his temples. When he faced me he looked like he had no ears at all. His cheeks and chin were blue. They would always be blue, no matter how many times a day he shaved. He wore a pale blue dress shirt, no tie, with the cuffs turned back showing a mat of black hair on his wrists and the backs of his hands, all but obscuring a tattoo on the right, the ornate cross of the Eastern Orthodox Church with turnips on the ends.

"Who's asking?" No discernible accent. I'd sort of been hoping for Taras Bulba.

I gave him a card.

"I'm helping out with the Gates investigation. I understand you worked with him here."

He finished reading and slid the card into his shirt pocket. "Just to talk to. I'm filling in for him because I know the machine. I programmed it."

"Gates did that, I heard."

"He installed it. It's not the same thing. The old one was in place since the seventies. The timing of the lights downtown was a disgrace, especially during rush hour. Since he knew so much about it, Gates got the job of monitoring the new machine — on the off chance it malfunctioned, which happened maybe twice a year. The rest of the time he sat here sucking up caffeine, like me."

"If he knew that much about it, why didn't he do the programming?"

"Different specialty. During high-traffic events, say, there's a high-rivalry school football game, a political rally, and some pimply boy band playing a concert, I come in and change the timing to keep things moving smoothly. Meanwhile someone like Gates sits here —"

"Sucking up caffeine. Sounds mind-numbing."

"Not to someone who busted his butt doing odd jobs to put himself through school. I'll still be paying off my student loan come the trumpet. Did you know the first car gets five seconds for the driver to make up his mind to go through the green, while all the rest get two? That's the brilliant sort of thinking that put Gates in this chair."

"Some guys got all the luck."

"Yeah. His parents weren't rich, but they put him through school on what they'd saved since he was in the womb, and because he had a degree in computer science he stepped right into this job still wearing his mortarboard. The city had just decided to junk the old computer when he came for his interview. He was the first through the door and they told everybody else to go home."

"You being one of them."

"Yeah, but I got a callback. They needed a

programmer."

"So it all worked out."

"Except the job doesn't pay as well."

"Mind telling me where you were New Year's Eve?"

White teeth showed in the blue lower half of his face.

"I was wondering when you'd get around to that. I was right here, checking the program for the annual drunks' parade. See, the rest of the year the lights go to flashers after midnight, but that's when things get lively on January first, so we chuck that. Someone has to make sure they turn green and yellow and red when they're supposed to. Gates had seniority, so he got the night off while I rang out the old with a pot of Folger's."

"Were you alone?"

"Just me and the security cameras at all the doors. Check the tapes. You won't find me ducking out before my shift ended at eight A.M."

"Okay. Thanks, Mr. Yako."

"Yako." He pronounced it with a short *a*. "I'm Ukrainian on my father's side, Russian on the other."

"There's a difference?"

He colored.

"Don't ask my father that question. Ukrainians are descended from Cossacks. Cossacks fought alongside Russia only when they were paid or when they could use the help. They didn't give a shit about fancy Easter eggs or Peter the Great setting fire to beards at Court."

I thanked him for the history lesson. "And thanks for the heads-up on those two seconds."

"You didn't hear it from me. I don't want to be responsible for another land rush." He scratched his stubble. "Who blew the whistle on me?"

I turned back from the door. "No one. We're just talking to everyone who knew the victim."

"The cops already did that. Why'd I have to go all over it again?"

"Consider it a callback." I left.

There was no point in checking with security. If the cameras had caught him sneaking out early, he'd already be in custody. Henty was too good to have overlooked it.

I knew about Ukrainians. I'd just wanted to see if he riled easily. Most killers do.

Six

"Walker?"

"That's what it says on the door."

"Huh?"

"I'm Walker. Please sit down, Mr. Adams."

Alvinus C. Adams tugged at the chair in front of the desk, lifting his heavy brow when it didn't budge.

"Just a precaution against bad breath," I said. "Nothing personal. I bolted it down years ago."

He lowered himself into it as if it were a steaming tub. Seated, he looked bigger than he had standing. His legs were short, bowed, and his work trousers bagged around them; childhood rickets, possibly. He looked too young for polio. I filed him on the sunny side of forty, with no gray in his black hair and his eyes around the irises as clear as egg whites. From the waist up he was built broad and solid, his face a mass of bony ridges with some old scar tissue; some fists had broken up on those rocks. He was clean-shaven, with muscular hands and square nails clipped or bitten short. He was dressed for manual labor, in blue twill and steel-toed boots. The red necktie looked out of place; but I remembered what he'd said about his reason for being in the city.

"How'd the job interview go?"

"Don't know yet. They're seeing other people, the man said. So I'm still looking and will be after they call me with the news. Or don't, which happens just as often."

"What do you do?"

"You name it. Forklift, power shovel, dozer, tractor-trailer. My driving record's clean as a colon flush and not a single accident on a worksite. So why see other people?"

I looked at the facial scars, the ones on his knuckles, and hazarded a guess.

Anyway it was a rhetorical question. "Anybody can rent an office in this town by the day, especially a dump like this. How I know you're the guy I axed about all over southeastern Michigan?"

I jerked a thumb over my shoulder at my license framed on the wall next to the window.

"That don't prove a thing. There's a shop in Port Huron where I can get a newspaper printed saying I was elected president."

"Anyone can be elected president. Anyone can't operate a bulldozer; or find a missing child. I can see you're a hard man to take in, Mr. Adams. A lot of guys who thought they could are probably still hearing bells." I lit a cigarette and tossed the pack his direction. He had a pack of his own in one flap pocket and the rectangular outline of a lighter in the other. "Let's break the law and smoke up some conversation."

After a moment he scooped up the pack, tapped one loose, and drew it from the pack by the lips. He started to put the pack on the desk.

"Keep it," I said. "Yours looks kind of flat."

"I wouldn't, but they're getting to be an investment." He found room for it in his pocket and buttoned the flap: the tidy type. "Thanks. This don't come out of the *re*-ward, does it?"

I studied his face, decided to chuckle. "No." I swiveled toward the safe that had brought over Queen Isabella's jewels, opened it, and broke out another hundred. I shut the door on the office bottle and the clean shirt I kept there in case I bled on the one I wore and spun the knob. At the bank, I'd taken the cash out of Florence Melville's check in fives, so there was a nice neat band around the bundle. I put it on the desk and stood the heavy rotary-dial phone on top of it.

"Not exactly ten thousand. But if I like what I hear, it's the first installment. Dazzle me."

"I was walking my dog in this Gates's neighborhood. I didn't know it was his neighborhood then, and I didn't know him from Pharaoh. I only put it together later when I saw the house on the news. About dark it was. There was a car parked in front of the place with the motor running: You can't miss that on a cold day, the exhaust comes thick out of the pipe. Man behind the wheel. I didn't think nothing of it; maybe he belonged to the house and was waiting for someone, his wife or someone, warming the motor while he waited. I can't afford that, gas costing what it does; but maybe he's got a job. Some folks still do, I guess."

I drew in smoke, let it out through my nose, watched it drift toward the window, said nothing. He lived alone, probably, just him and the dog. No one to talk to but the dog.

"Didn't think nothing of it, till he saw me, that is. Right away he flips the visor down in front of his face, pulls away from the curb, and drives off, turning his head away from me like he's looking for an address on the other side of the street."

Silence creaked. The lights dimmed, then brightened; Karaoke Press had opened for business. I wondered again just what an e-book was and if there was any work in it for me.

"That's it?" I said.

"Yeah. The sun was going down behind him, you see. He had no reason to turn down that visor except to cover his face; and if he was looking for an address, why'd he stop there?"

"Read his directions. Look at a city map. Use his cell, the way you're supposed to, not while driving. Blow his nose, which takes two hands. That's just off the top of my head. People stop their cars and pull over for all sorts of reasons or none at all."

He ditched the cigarette in the tray. "They don't hide their faces unless they're up to something."

"Better," I said. "But not ten thousand dollars' worth. Not a hundred bucks' worth either. Gas money, maybe, from here back to the Heights. I made a resolution this year to take better care of my fellow man, but the expiration date always runs out about this time in February."

"What if I gave you a license number?"

"Better yet. If it leads to something promising, I'd consider staking you to the hundred. That'd give you something to build on if the ten grand comes into play." I slid over the telephone pad and dealt myself a pencil.

"V-A-L. I didn't get the rest."

I wrote. "Michigan plate?"

"Yeah. Blue and white, anyway; none of that vanity bullshit."

"It's a start. Make and model?"

"One of those midsize jobs, looks like a shucked oyster. I can't tell 'em apart no more."

"What'd the guy look like?"

"I didn't see his face, like I said."

"How'd you know it was a man?"

"If it was a woman she should try out for the Lions, he was that wide crosst the shoulders. Had him on a quilted coat, some kind of hat; sock hat, I think, no fancy fluff. It was a man, I'm sure of that."

"This was New Year's Eve?"

"Night before."

I pushed the pad away.

"No gas money for you. Gates was alive the night before, the next day too. Whoever clocked him did it between when he left the office New Year's Eve and midnight New

Year's Day, or shortly after."

"You ever hear of casing a place?"

"Look, Mr. Adams, I'll see it's run out. If it looks good, someone will be in touch with you. That's a promise. My license comes with a stiff bond. I can't afford to make pledges I can't keep."

He stood up all of a piece, fists balled at his side. I drew my feet under me and leaned forward in my chair, lifting the telephone, standard and all. It was my best chance to block one of those fists if it went airborne.

I'd forgotten about the hundred. He misunderstood the action. He didn't reach for it, but he opened his hands and let them hang.

I opened the belly drawer and slid the bundle of bills into it. His fingers twitched, but I felt better with the drawer open. The Smith & Wesson Chief's Special lay inside.

He couldn't see it from his angle, but all the starch went out of him then; he was a proud man, a man out of work, a hard man who'd taken so many punches from someone out of his reach there wasn't much use in being proud or hard. He nodded and turned away, dragging his feet now in their armored boots.

"What's the breed?" I asked.

He stopped, turned an uncomprehending face on me.

"Your dog."

"Chow." His expression lightened a little. "Prettiest little chow you ever did see. Smarter'n any crew I ever worked with. Ten years old, thinks she's still a puppy. When's the last time you saw a seventy-year-old jump his own height over a low branch?"

I tugged four fives out of the bundle and shoved the drawer shut. I stood and held them out.

He shook his head. "Uh-uh. Unless it's against the ten thousand."

"That'd be stringing you along. It's a loan. Thanks for coming down."

"Mister, there's no down from where I am. And a loan's only a loan if you think you can pay it back." He was looking me in the eye now. The bills in my hand didn't exist.

I folded them, stuck them inside my breast pocket, and tore the sheet with the license number on it off the top. On the next sheet I scribbled a name, tore off that sheet, and held it out.

"This man works in the City-County Building. They call it the Coleman A. Young Municipal Center now. He's in Human Resources."

"Janitor?"

"No such luck. There's a high turnover in security guards there. That's because the pay's low. On the other hand the hours are long and the health plan wouldn't keep your dog in shots. Got a record?"

"I got probation when I was thirteen. Possession of pot, four ounces."

"Just don't carry it to work, okay? I'm running out of character references."

"Why the boost? You don't know me."

"I got a break recently I didn't deserve. I'm paying down the debt."

After he left, taking the sheet with him, I put the money back in the safe, locked up, and stopped at a carryout restaurant on the way home; one of those places where you had to decide what kind of meat went into the sandwich, what kind of bread to put it between, whether you wanted it heated up, what to put on it, and what to drink with it. That exhausted every last gig in my dial-up brain.

I ate in the kitchen and tuned in a game show for company, but the host was smarmy and the contestants had all the intelligence of a traffic barrel. It was lonely with the set off, so I put Kay Starr on the turntable. All I heard was clicks and pops with some verses in between, and they sounded like a ripsaw going through knotty pine. I swapped Kay for something more contemporary, built a drink, a silly thing of gin with some mint leaves left over from a recipe that hadn't been worth the prep. The drink wasn't either; it tasted like Christmas punch marinated in last year's fruitcake. I poured the rest into the sink and switched to Scotch.

I wasn't celebrating; not the fact that I had work or my own damn good samaritanship. If Adams got the job, he'd probably lose his temper sometime, deck a union lobbyist, get himself tanked, and cuss me out for providing the bad break. I drank because I hadn't had a drink since beer for breakfast.

The ice jingled in the glass. I had a first-class case of the shakes. What I really wanted was a pill.

I got as far as the telephone to call my teenage connection. The card belonging to the private therapist was still there poking out from under the standard. I finished my drink over the *Free Press,* reading about a city councilman under hack for inappropriate relations with a teenage boy; had another, listened to some more music, and went to bed. They say we dream every time we sleep, but as usual, they lie — a fact for which I was grateful. I'd had my share of nightmares in rehab.

Seven

Operator: *Sheriff's tip line. What's your information?*

Caller: *I know who killed that Gates guy.*

Operator: *Yes, sir.*

Caller: *I don't need a reward.*

Operator: *That's refreshing.*

Caller: *It's Fred Gudgast, works quality control at Ford River Rouge.*

Operator: *Why do you think he killed Mr. Gates?*

Caller: *He's murdered at least three people at the plant and got away with it. He's one of those serial killers, you know?*

Operator: *Have you any evidence?*

Caller: *He's a miserable piece of shit, how's that for evidence?*

Operator: *Does Mr. Gudgast even know Mr. Gates?*

Caller: *Serial killers don't have to know*

their victims.
So you're just guessing?
Fuck you, lady.
Thank you for calling.

I let it go on like that while I washed out my coffee cup, then turned off the tape player.

You had to feel sorry for operators of 911 and tip lines:

"What's your emergency?"
"I can't remember where I parked my car in the lot."
"Try pushing the button on your key fob, ma'am."
"I can't; I lost my keys."

"What's your emergency?"
"I got my hand stuck in a vending machine."
"How'd that happen, sir?"
"Fucking thing stole my dollar."

"What's your emergency?"
"This car in front of me's had his blinker on for three miles."
"Why not pass it?"
"Can't. What if he decides to pull out finally?"

"What's your emergency?"
"What's the capital of Brazil?"
"Young man, get off the line at once."

"What's your emergency?"
"I flipped the self-cleaning lever by mistake and now my chicken's burning."

"What's your emergency?"
"My next-door neighbor never closes his curtains. Every night I can see everything he's got; believe me, it's no treat."

"What's your emergency?"
"I can't keep the raccoons out of my garbage."

"What's your emergency?'
"These directions don't make any sense."

"What's your emergency?"
"I need the number of the Wal-Mart pharmacy."

"What's your emergency?"
"How do I program my TiVo?"

"What's your emergency?"
"I'm lost in a corn maze."

And people wondered why they ran out of sympathy.

Stay away from the wife, Ray Henty had said. But that was when my duties were restricted to playing deejay for people with hunches and grudges to unload. I got the number from the file and called it.

Donald Gates answered from beyond the grave: "No one can come to the phone right now. Please leave a message." At least I assumed it was him. I cradled the receiver and left for Iroquois Heights.

The dead man smiled down at me from the billboard at the first exit. The city limits sign still read:

IROQUOIS HEIGHTS
HOME OF THE WARRIORS
YOU ARE UNDER SURVEILLANCE

I wondered how long it would be before I could cross that border without feeling like I was stepping into the O.K. Corral with a cap pistol in my holster.

The house was painted lime green, which somehow managed to look like the only color that made sense. It was a Wright knockoff, fresh enough for the junipers planted out front to resemble an architect's drawing, bunches of broccoli easy to maintain. It was an old neighborhood, with some of the prewar saltboxes still standing on small lots among newer, larger houses, all well-kept; the local ordinances and the Homeowners' Property Association were plenty clear on that subject.

"Mister? Are you looking for Mrs. Gates?"

I'd rung the bell and was about to push the button again when the woman called to me from a driveway across the street. She wore a cloth coat over a housedress, a scarf covering her hair and tied under her chin, and held that day's rolled edition of the local paper. She looked about fifty, and like her house, kept well.

I threw away the cigarette I'd just lit. "Do you know where she is?"

"Belle Isle."

"What's on Belle Isle this time of year?"

"Homeless. Detroit lets them set up their tents there in the winter. Amelie helps out, bringing them food and blankets and whatever else they need."

"I heard she's the generous type."

"I keep telling her she's not helping them at all. Some of those people are in their twenties, and not handicapped so far as I can tell. Do you know what McDonald's pays? Better than my Chester ever made driving a bread truck for Wonder. In a couple of months they'd save enough to put down a deposit on an apartment. But they're not about to go to work until people stop giving them handouts."

"I guess it helps to stay occupied, after what happened."

"You know about that?" The frown she'd worn for the twentysomethings on the island turned down farther. "If you're looking for a reward, you came to the wrong place. It's her church putting it up."

"I've got other business with Mrs. Gates. Do you know how long she'll be gone?"

"All day, probably. When you waste time on a bunch like that, you waste a lot of it."

She went back inside. I groped for another cigarette. I could have been the murderer, for all she knew; but she only had time to think about the people who wouldn't flip burgers for a utility flat in the city, and she didn't like wasting it.

A gust caught the Cutlass broadside as I drove over the MacArthur Bridge from Jefferson. It packed a wallop and I had to clamp both hands on the wheel to avoid drifting into the opposite lane, where a delivery van was headed back toward the mainland on the double. Apart from that I had the span all to myself.

Lake St. Clair was gray as shale and looked about the same consistency. A frozen haze lay on the other side, behind which someone had built a scale model of Windsor, Ontario, out of lead. No telling what was going on there after sixteen straight days without sunshine; Canadians are coy about their suicides.

I never seem to visit Belle Isle in nice weather, when the picnic ground's in use and the culture crowd is drifting in and out of the Dossin Marine Museum with its dioramas of bootlegging boats and artifacts from the *Edmund Fitzgerald.* Admiral Perry's guns still guard the place, their muzzles spiked with twenty years' worth of birds' nests and exhausted condoms. I could have used the guns the time I almost left my brains on the softball diamond, soaked to my knees with snow. A lifetime ago. Someone's parole would be coming up for review.

There was talk of turning the island over to Lansing and making it a state park; anything to avoid paying for the upkeep. Everything on it needed painting or patching or tearing down and burning up.

Well, the same was true of the city where I work. It was rotting from the top down and from the inside out like Dutch elm. The politicians let the homeless live in tents on public property and boarded up the houses they didn't tear down.

I turned on a classical station to stop that train of thought. It could only lead to another three weeks in the Amy Winehouse Memorial Spa.

They'd picked the ball field to pitch their tents; a little Hooverville, only with nylon instead of canvas and space heaters powered by borrowed generators making a racket like billiard balls bouncing off the skulls of pro wrestlers. This was where all the folks who sold dead flowers on exit ramps and stood on street corners holding cardboard signs made from the north walls of their houses came to rest. Campfires were burning, against ordinance. I smelled Spam frying, coffee boiling, and cannabis. Joan Baez was driving Old Dixie down one last time on a portable CD player. Hip-hop vomited out of someone's earbuds, loud enough to cause a brain hemorrhage to the one wearing them. It seemed no one wanted to bother to learn the harmonica anymore.

I parked and approached a group of men and women constructing a bonfire on the pitcher's mound with chairs and mattresses. There's nothing like the smell of urine cooking to take your mind off the cold.

"Who's in charge?"

A man who was all white-stubbled chin and hook nose leaned a maple headboard against his knee and pulled a filthy scarf away from the bottom half of his face. He'd used his teeth to open bottles. "All of us are, brother. The island's a socialist state."

"Okay, Woody. That's a shore-bound breeze wafting from Canada at about a thousand miles an hour. Where you going to sleep after you burn down all the tents?"

"What do you care, brother? What's anybody care what happens to us no more?"

"You know what McDonald's is paying by the hour?"

"Fuck you."

"I don't either, but everyone else seems to. Happen to know where Amelie Gates is working today?"

"Don't know nobody by that name."

"There a volunteer tent?"

He blew his nose on the sleeve of his camo coat. He was a colorful character. "That white one there, up by the fountain."

"Much obliged, Woody."

"The name's Howard. Who's this Woody you got me confused with?"

"A guy who sang about rock-candy mountains and jails made out of tin. You ought to look him up on your smart phone."

"Got one, wise guy." He dug it out of a pocket and shook it in my face.

"Okay, Howard. No offense meant."

He was poking at his phone in the rear-view. If he dug up Woody Woodpecker first, I was going to get my car keyed.

The bust of Dante Alighieri topped a marble pedestal on the main drag, wearing a cabbage on his head. What the author of *The Divine Comedy* was doing in that location was anybody's guess. He didn't look any too pleased to be there.

The tent erected nearby was really a canopy, stretched across the tops of aluminum poles secured with ropes and stakes. A long trestle table ran down the center with clam chowder, dumplings, scalloped potatoes, and shaved ham staying warm in aluminum containers above Sterno. A bevy of women wearing aprons over topcoats and earflapped caps kept the containers filled from an army of gas grills at the back of the tent and ladled the contents onto paper plates for those who couldn't help themselves. I got in line behind a red-haired kid with wads of Kleenex stuck under a pair of stereo earphones, but I didn't pick up a plate.

"Is one of you ladies Amelie Gates?"

"That's me."

A woman behind the scalloped potatoes swept a sleeve across her brow. Her French accent was as out of place as Dante.

I didn't know what to expect; a drawn-looking woman, maybe, with pinched nostrils and dark circles under her eyes. Maybe someday I'll learn not to form conclusions ahead of evidence, and then my detective training will begin.

The Widow Gates was small, but built to proportion, with a small upturned nose, eyes like black olives, and a delicate mouth set in a small square chin. Her figure was indeterminate under the apron and quilted coat. The checked hunter's cap covered her hair, but it would be as dark as her eyes and probably short; I have fixed ideas about Gallic women. The smile she wore to greet me looked genuine, and entirely without regret. But everyone mourns in his or her own way. They don't all tear at their faces and scrape their knees throwing themselves on the coffin at graveside.

"You look like you could use a break."

"We all do. What makes me special? Where's your plate?" She looked doubtfully at my suit and warm overcoat.

"I'm not hungry," I lied; the fare smelled like a Nordic feast, and I hadn't eaten since Subway last night. "I'm here on business, if you've got a minute."

She glanced sideways at her fellow volunteers. "That's just about what I've got, Mr. — ?"

"Walker." I held out my card. "I'm trying to find out who knows who killed Donald Gates."

EIGHT

The smile faltered a little when she read the card. She turned to the woman standing next to her. "Beverly, can you look after my station for a few minutes?"

The woman nodded, and moved into the middle position between dumplings and potatoes. Amelie Gates ditched her apron and we left the canopy and sat down at an unoccupied picnic table. She was sweating a little from standing over the heated dishes; she unbuttoned her coat and let it hang free. She was slender and moderately busty.

"Those billboards were a good idea," I said. "People drive by them every day. They stick."

"I can only take credit for the line. Putting up signs was Michel's idea."

"Michel?"

"Our — my son. He's ten. He remembered when our cat went missing two years ago, and we put up posters all over the neighborhood with its picture. I was crying at the time, over so little news from the sheriff's department. He's a sweet boy. Making the arrangements kept us busy and took our minds off our grief. He helped me pick out the photograph. It's one of my favorites; I didn't know, when I took it — it would be —" Her chin quivered. She looked down at her hands folded on the table.

"Did you find the cat?"

"No. Does anyone ever?"

"Once, anyway. It was found in perfect health, licking the condensation off the wall of a luggage compartment in an airplane a thousand miles away from home. You never know about these things."

"The hell with the cat. He barfed all over my best sofa."

"Tell me about Donald. Lieutenant Henty said you met in Quebec."

"My father was caretaker of a hunting lodge. He still is. The place Donald used to hunt was bought by a corporation and reserved for executive retreats. I worked the counter, checking in guests and seeing to their comfort. He was cute. He had a start on a beard — it's kind of a uniform of the sport — but it was coming in sort of sparse and ginger-colored. It made him look younger than he was rather than the other way around. I was — I guess you could say I was —" She groped through her command of the language.

"Smitten."

She brightened. "Yes. It's an old-fashioned word, isn't it? You don't hear it much anymore."

"In a few years half the world won't be able to understand the other half. What did he hunt?"

"Elk." She shook her head, still smiling. "He wasn't very good at it, I'm afraid. In eight years he never shot one. Do you know what I think? I think he had lots of chances but never took them. It was just an excuse to get away with friends and commune with nature."

"What were his friends like?"

"I never really got to know them. He'd had some of them since high school, and they were scattered all over the United States. They only got together during the season, and he stopped going after Michel was born. The trips were too expensive to justify, with a family to look after."

"I'd like the names of his friends, if you can get them."

"I suppose I can. He kept an address book. Why?"

"I used to hunt deer with my father

upstate. He always said if you really want to know who your friends are, you should spend three days with them in a hunting camp. The veneer wears off quick."

"Why would someone kill Donald? That's the question I want to ask when they find who did it."

I lit a cigarette, mainly to cover the smell of warm food drifting my way. I don't eat breakfast and I didn't want to chisel off the chronically hungry. "You seem pretty sure they'll find him."

"I have to. It's all I have, apart from my son. I lost the baby, you know."

"I heard. I'm sorry. What do you think of the reward your church put up?"

She looked me in the eye. "It's a damn nuisance. People keep calling the house with what they think they know. I tell them to call the sheriff, or the church. I've tried to persuade the Reverend Melville to withdraw it. She says that's up to the person who offered it, and he's adamant. Do you know who he is?"

"Do you?"

"No. I think if I could just talk to him, make him see the reward is actually getting in the way of the investigation, he'll see my side. But Florence won't budge. Budge, yes?"

"Yes. I think your English is better than you make out. Pretending to have to think about what someone's saying to you is a good way to buy time while you think of what to say back."

Up close her eyes weren't black at all, but a deep shade of brown.

"Do you always say exactly what's on your mind?"

"When I think it'll save time." I pointed to the pocket where she'd put my card. "You can get me on my cell when you have the names of Donald's hunting buddies. Men open up among themselves more than you might think, especially over drinks and euchre."

"Euchre?"

"Card game: one of those cuss-and-slam-down-a-card affairs. It's not played much outside the Midwest."

"He never mentioned it. Do you know how to play?"

"I'm rusty, but I could brush up."

"Will you teach me? I've been looking for something to occupy my thoughts since the billboards."

"I'd be glad to; just as soon as I brush up on it myself."

She smiled, and I saw the pain then.

"I'll hold you to that. It's the quiet that

sets in, you know? After the ceremony and the good wishes and the offers to help are over and done with. It's one of the reasons I'm here feeding strangers while my son is being looked after by other strangers."

"How are they getting along?"

"Children are resilient. Anyway, that's what everyone keeps telling me, or almost everyone. Michel's teacher thinks he should be in counseling. I don't know. What do you think?"

"What I think doesn't count. I've never had children."

"That's refreshing. You're the first person I've spoken to on the subject who hasn't had an opinion."

I was still looking for something in that for me when she moved on.

"Not just yet, I think. He knows he can talk to me about anything, when he's ready. I hope that's the right decision. We read all the books, when I was pregnant the first time. One says keep after them, another says let them alone. The authors all have the same letters after their names. I always look at their biographies, to see if they're actually someone's parent, but that doesn't tell me much. It isn't like studying for a test, where there are right and wrong answers, nothing in between."

"That only applies to tests."

She worked her hands; strong hands, the nails well kept, but not to the point of glamour. "Mr. Walker, do you think you can find who did this?"

I jumped on that one; something inside my field.

"Chances are someone will. Murders get solved as a rule. Most of them right on the spot, with the killer standing over the victim and his confession all ready. The problem ones take time, so that when there's a solution the press has lost interest. Then it shows up after the weather report, when people stop reading to get to the comics.

"It might be somebody you know," I added. "An uncle, a shirttail relative, the oh-so-helpful next-door neighbor who posts all the signs; he's the one the police concentrate on. It happens. You have to be prepared for that, along with what comes with it."

The woman who'd taken over her station came out from under the canopy and leaned down close to her.

"I'm sorry to interrupt, dear. Traffic's picking up."

"I'll be there in a minute."

When we were alone again Amelie said, "I can't imagine anyone I know could be responsible. But even if it's someone I thought was a friend, it's better than wondering if anyone I pass on the street is the one who did it."

She stood.

"Thank you for coming. I feel better knowing Don hasn't slipped through some crack in the system."

"There are plenty of those, but it doesn't happen as often as people think."

"Don't forget about euchre."

"I won't."

I took the hand she offered me, let go of it, and left. There wasn't a thing to be gained by telling her that the solution's almost always as bad as the problem.

NINE

On the way back to the office I called the sheriff's substation in Iroquois Heights, but the dispatcher or whoever I got said Ray Henty was out on a call. I left my name and the partial license plate number I'd gotten from Alvinus C. Jones. The car it belonged to had been hanging around Gates's house a day early, but there might have been something in it. Anyway the lieutenant had eight times as many legs as I had to run such things down.

I didn't have to turn away any desperate heiresses waiting for me in the arid little reception room. Nobody sapped me when I unlocked and opened the door to the think tank. I'd had enough experience with the latter to welcome the silence, but not nearly enough of the former.

It was a little chilly. I twisted the thermostat. The elf who lived inside the radiator tapped the pipes with his little hammer and the furnace in the basement came back from its break with a shudder that shook the building. The out-of-state conglomination that owned the place had given Rosecranz a manual override, along with strict instructions to keep track of when the tenants were out.

I set the swivel chair to squeaking, dialed city hall in the Heights, and asked for the head of traffic control. I listened to three minutes of non-Christian Christmas carols, then a woman's voice with a rusty wire running through it came on the line.

I said I was an independent investigator working with the sheriff's department on the Donald Gates case, and asked if it was possible for someone monitoring the traffic lights to work from home. That would be one explanation why Yuri Yako hadn't shown up on security cameras leaving the building.

"Not possible," said the woman. "The firewalls would prevent access except through the mainframe itself, and the passwords change by the week."

"Thanks. It was just a hunch." If Yako had crooked the system to give himself an alibi, he would have had to be photographed coming into the building for his shift; Henty would have checked that. I started to hang up.

"By the way, our monitor didn't come to work today. Is he being detained?"

I tightened my grip on the handset. "Did you try Yako at home?"

"We don't need an independent investigator to suggest that, Mr. Walker. We rang him several times, at home and on his cell. He never picked up, and our messages haven't been returned. Since he was Gates's replacement, we didn't have time to train anyone to take his place, so we had to transfer a programmer from headquarters. Traffic lights aren't his specialty, so we've had yellow flashers going all day. It's a mess. If you take my advice, you'll stay away from downtown."

"I'm thinking you don't want that to get back to the chamber of commerce."

"I really don't care. I've given notice. Last year, my husband was murdered for his wallet. The year before that, my son lost an eye trying to keep his running shoes. Those were bad neighborhoods. When that element infiltrates the place where I work, I'm out of here."

While she was talking I flipped open the sheriff's department reports, made sure I had Yako's personal contact numbers, and thanked her. She hung up in the middle of it.

The Ukrainian-Russian didn't answer his landline or cell. I disconnected from the answering devices and got back into my winter gear. I was going to have to brave those flashers after all.

He had an apartment just off the zigzag main drag in a building intended for student housing, eight stories of what looked like graphite, with vacancy signs in most of the windows. Some financial affairs manager at the county community college had tried to fix a sluggish economy with a steep hike in tuition, and now he was wearing a paper hat in a chain restaurant in Port Huron. The apartments were new, as was most of the construction in the neighborhood, thanks to an impromptu demolition by a fleet of trucks a few years back. I couldn't claim noninvolvement in that. I cranked a fistful of quarters into a meter that still bore the name of a neighboring city embossed on the steel: The old administration had snapped them up after every other place in the area ripped them out to encourage business downtown. No one keeps track of loose change when the FBI is patting down half the elected officials for tens of thousands.

I buzzed the manager's apartment, showed my ID, and gave him my spiel. He scratched his scalp under a lifelike hairpiece and got his passkey. We rode up in an elevator that smelled of fresh paint and made as much noise as a kitten playing with a piece of string.

Yako's name occupied a black rectangular insert next to a door with 4A on it in brushed brass. The manager knocked, waited, knocked again. "Mr. Yako?"

No sound came from inside. He knocked a third time, said "Mr. Yako?" again. When he raised his fist for another cycle, I closed a hand on it. When I gave it back he used the passkey. He started to go in. I shouldered him aside, drawing the Chief's Special from the holster under my coattail. I went in.

I didn't do the two-handed thing you see on TV; my old partner had said if that made sense, guns would come with two handles, like a weed-whacker. I circled a living room that wasn't any messier or tidier than it had to be, with a flat-screen TV mounted on a wall, a smattering of magazines, some sleek furniture the manufacturer couldn't be bothered to assemble itself, and half an inch of pale green carpet pasted to a subfloor that sprang underfoot like the plywood it was. The manager stood in the doorway, watching me and going to town on that dry patch under his toupee. It hardly seemed worth the trouble; he didn't look even a bit like Brad Pitt. I didn't stumble over any bodies and there were no curtains on the windows for a pair of shoe tips to poke out of. I wondered just when all the romance had worn off the profession.

"Don't look like he's here," said the manager.

I gave that all the attention it needed and checked the bathroom. Yako squeezed his toothpaste from the middle of the tube and unrolled his toilet paper up from under. I liked him less and less.

I didn't like the bedroom even more. He'd flung his clothes into a pile on a chintz-covered slipper chair and turned down the page corners in a slipshod stack of racy paperbacks on the nightstand. In the stir of air when the door opened, a dust bunny rolled out like a tumbleweed from under the bed. It was big enough to let loose in a dog park.

But it wasn't his shoddy housekeeping I didn't care for. The bed was made, hospital corners and all, under a green foam spread turned down at the top as neatly as a show handkerchief.

"Hey!" The manager had followed me as far as the doorway, but that was the only objection he made as I put away my revolver and tore loose the bedding, mattress pad and all. The mattress looked clean except for a few shed hairs.

I slid both hands under the bottom and heaved it over. A corner clipped the paper shade on the lamp on the nightstand, knocking it crooked and tilting it off its base, but the lamp settled back down without overturning.

I didn't pay it any attention, and neither did the manager. We were looking at a bloodstain the size of a throw rug on that side of the mattress.

The drawer in the nightstand was empty except for a pair of drugstore reading glasses and a squat semiautomatic pistol. Wrapping my hand in my handkerchief, I picked it up, sniffed vanilla-scented oil, and turned it to tip light inside the muzzle.

"If I knew he had that, I'd've told him to get rid of it or find another place to live. I don't like guns or the people that use them." The manager frowned at my revolver.

"It didn't do him any good. Dust in the barrel."

It was an unfamiliar piece. I looked for the name of the manufacturer. The characters were Cyrillic.

I asked the manager if he knew Russian.

"Just my way around a bottle of vodka. Think it was communists?"

"If it was, they didn't use this gun." I put it back in the position I'd found it.

"We better call the cops." He made for the telephone on the nightstand.

I blocked his path. "You don't want those print boys mad at you." I got out my cell and went to the window. I had to change positions three times before I found a signal.

The manager waited until I finished talking to the sheriff's sergeant. "I was out of work three months before I got this job. Guess I'll be looking again."

"Did you kill him?"

"Brother, I didn't even know him."

"Not much of an alibi in this town."

A set of tires squished to a stop in front of a fire hydrant four stories down. A star was stenciled on the hood of the car. Ray Henty got out.

Ten

"I think we can safely call this a homicide," Henty said.

"That, or somebody's in deep shit for slaughtering a hog inside the city limits."

The comedian was a sheriff's detective named Benteen, one of the younger breed, who wore his shirttail out under a gray suitcoat, no hat or overcoat. He shaved his temples so that his head looked like a mushroom growing straight up from his collar.

The lieutenant turned his back on the stained sheet and bent over the windowsill.

"Offhand I'd say the body didn't go out this way. No rope marks. I'd like to think our local criminal element's too smart to dump one out freestyle."

"Make a hell of a smack," said the detective. "Not to mention the mess."

"No wonder they promoted you to plainclothes. What'd you say to Yako?" Henty was looking at me now.

"Where was he, and yada-yada," I said. "First pass stuff. He didn't rattle."

"Someone did. Let's ring Detroit in on this. They've got more experience."

"They've got their hands full with another FBI investigation," Benteen said. "I'd like a crack at this solo."

"I thought the feebs closed that down sometime back," the lieutenant said.

"This one's new. I've got a girl with Dispatch there. Couple of beat cops are under hack for moonlighting. Not ripe enough yet for public consumption."

"That's pissant stuff. Internal business."

"Did I mention they were heavy-lifting for the mob?"

"No, Benteen, you didn't. Which mob?"

"Search me, L.T. They're keeping it wrapped tight."

"Ukrainian."

This voice belonged to a fresh card in the deal. A trim young woman stood in the bedroom doorway, wearing a tan suede coat with fake fur trim and a red knitted hat that flopped over on one side like an artist's in a cartoon, ankle boots on her small feet. Her presence on a crime scene did wonders for it, like a spray of fresh flowers on a city bus.

Benteen stepped toward her. "This is a

closed set, lady. No civilians allowed."

She stopped him with a practiced wrist flip, showing off a gold star pinned to a leather folder.

"Mary Ann Thaler, Deputy U.S. Marshal. Hello, Amos. I heard you retired."

"I tried. Math didn't work out. I thought you'd be moled in deep with Al-Qaeda by now."

"They don't take women unless they're combustible. There wasn't much room for advancement. I'm with WitSec now."

"What's WitSec?"

"Witness Security."

"I thought that was WitPro: Witness Protection."

"That was two name-changes ago. Try and keep up."

Henty said, "Start again. I want to get this clever bullshit on my smart phone. What's the Marshals' Service want with a dead computer programmer in the Heights?"

She glanced toward the manager, lurking outside in the living room.

"Not here. You boys done playing detective?"

Car doors slammed, a volley. Henty looked out the window. "Forensics outran the uniforms. I'm scheduling drills."

"Good thinking. If there's anything we

don't need in a hurry, it's the ghouls." Benteen scowled at Thaler. "Washington taking over?"

She smiled. "Assisting; now isn't that a friendlier way of putting it?"

It wasn't my first time in that office. The last time, a chief had been sitting behind the plain desk, playing with a set of brass knuckles that hadn't always been used as a paperweight. Last I'd heard he was wearing an electric anklet in the prison town of Milan.

The bulletin board with its album of plug-uglies and their aliases was gone, also the large-scale city map and confiscated weapons in a glass display case. The original decorator had worked from pictures taken in J. Edgar Hoover's office in Washington; the one he used for work, not the plush barn where he'd greeted the press. The government green hid under several fresh coats of beige paint, waiting to claw its way through, the way it always did, but for now the place might have belonged to a branch bank manager or some other midlevel executive who didn't plan to occupy it long enough to stamp it with his personality. Henty's wife smiled from a frame standing on the desk and his autographed poster of Gordie Howe hung on the wall above one of the athlete's old wooden hockey sticks.

"Stop fidgeting," the lieutenant said.

"Sorry." I sat down. "I was trying not to trip over my old dead brain cells."

Thaler said, "I'd consider it a favor if your detective sat this one out."

Benteen stiffened. "What about this character?"

She brushed me lightly with her cool brown stare.

"I know him. He doesn't have a girlfriend with the Detroit Police Department."

"Got your number." Henty's grin was wolfish. "Go play Clue."

He almost slammed the door going out. At the last second he thought better of it and eased it into the frame.

The lieutenant sat back in his quilted chair. "I inherited him. The sheriff wanted a liaison man who knew the old department, and his record's clean. When you never do anything, you never do anything wrong. Soon as I'm settled I'll palm him off on headquarters."

"I studied your record," Thaler said. "You've done plenty, and most of it right."

"G'wan with you. How'd you tumble to this so quick? Yako's name didn't go out over the air."

"His address did. We set him up in that apartment and got him the programming job with the city."

"Who'd he roll over on?" I asked.

"Big fish in California named Igorov. Yako's real name was Crowley. We let him keep the Yuri; it's common enough in that culture, and cuts down the odds of blowing your cover when somebody calls you by your first name."

"What's wrong with John Smith?" said Henty. "I don't mean to tell you your business, but isn't it risky to hang a name like Yako on a Ukrainian you're hiding from the Ukrainian mob?"

She looked at me. "You've seen him. Would you try to pass him off as Angus MacLanahan?"

"Don't drag me into it. I'm *suis generis.*"

She returned her attention to Henty.

"You know how crooks think. Wouldn't you pay a little more attention to every John Smith and Robert Miller you meet, especially when he looks like the love child of Boris Badenov and Miss Kazakhstan 1988? The metro area's crawling with Poles, Albanians, Croats, and Serbs; not to mention third-generation Americans whose great-grandparents skinny-dipped in the Black Sea. If we put him in Topeka he'd stand out like a bowl of borscht at a St. Patrick's Day dinner."

"Worked out swell, didn't it? I guess Ivan the Ripper read 'The Purloined Letter.' "

"The service can't be held responsible for the bad choices made by its charges. I'm proceeding on the theory Crowley/Yako killed Donald Gates to swing himself a promotion and his old friends in the outfit took him out, either because of old business or to sever any connection with a high-profile murder that could bring it down coast to coast. We could never prove it, but we're sure he did some wet work in California on top of the drug rap the DEA hung on him."

"You can't prove he did it here either, if that security-camera alibi holds water." I looked at Henty, who nodded.

"It does. Yuri shows up coming in for his shift and leaving when it was over, after Gates's time of death. Nothing in between."

"What do they use, disc or tape?"

"Disc."

"Some improvements aren't. He's a computer geek, Lieutenant. Don't you think he could hack into the surveillance program and erase himself from the record, or substitute a recording from another day and change the time-stamp?"

"I didn't. But I do now."

"The service would like to borrow the discs. We've got some pretty smart cookies in the District who can tell if they've been tampered with."

"Sure. If I say no you'll just sweet-talk a judge like you're sweet-talking me and come back with a warrant."

She smiled. "I knew those commendations were for real. Walker."

"No."

"I haven't asked the question yet."

"I know. I wanted to save the taxpayers time and money."

"Walker's working for the sheriff's department as a contract laborer," Henty said. "Running down anonymous tips."

"Aw. And me with a speech all prepared."

Thaler said, "I've heard it. Who tipped you Yako was dead?"

"I'm not sure he is dead. I talked to him yesterday. When I called with a follow-up question, the city drone I talked to said he hadn't been in today, so I went to see him at home. I found a nasty linen stain and called the sheriff's substation instead of Martha Stewart. It could be anyone's blood until the whiz kids finish straining and spinning it."

"You tossed the place without a warrant?"

"I don't have any experience tossing places with one. Anyway, I got the building manager to let me in."

"Who put you onto Yako in the first place?"

"It was anonymous, like the lieutenant said."

"I'm not a District dope. Did you forget I worked Felony Homicide for five years in Detroit? We knew who was calling before there was such a thing as caller ID, which by the way anyone can get around by punching star sixty-seven; but not our system. Anonymous is for *Bartlett's Quotations.*" She opened a red leather handbag, extracted a pocket gadget, and diddled the keys. "Was the name Roy Thompson? Maintenance worker in the city traffic building."

"No." It was refreshing, telling a cop the truth.

She made a scrolling motion. She kept her nails short, with clear polish. "His wife, then. Carol."

"Can you play solitaire on that thing?"

"Nice try. It was her, wasn't it?"

"What the hell. It's in the file. Her story's hearsay. You need to talk to Roy if you need evidence. I didn't, just to ask Yako some questions."

"She's the logical alternative, as next of kin."

A sheet of ice wrapped itself around my face.

"I never liked that phrase, Deputy. It's like 'personal effects.' Only the dead have them."

"Then you won't like where this conversation is going. That's how I got here so quick; I was on my way to talk to his hometown cops when Yako's address came up on the scanner. Roy drove to Detroit last night to drink with some friends. At two this morning, he wandered out of the bar smack in front of a car going far too fast for the conditions. It kept going."

Eleven

It had started raining, what we in the rust belt call a "wintry mix": part monsoon, part blizzard, with a pinch of the Aleutians. Japanese auto engineers traveled across half the world to collect, analyze, and try to duplicate it on their test grounds. All they have to deal with over there are hurricanes, earthquakes, tidal waves, and Godzilla.

"We invented hit-and-run here," I said. "First cars, then hit-and-run, then carjacking. Oddly enough, most of them seem to take place just after the bars close."

"Witnesses said Thompson did most of the weaving. He bounced off walls on both sides of the street, clear up the block, like the ball in a pinball machine."

I said, "You're too young to know what that is, but okay."

"I'm older than I look. The car missed him twice, bumping over both curbs, until they connected. The driver was in such a hurry to leave he ran over him for good measure."

"Any of these witnesses get the plate?"

She scrolled again. I held my breath for no good reason. "Nope."

I exhaled. Did I think it would start with V-A-L? It's never that tidy. I looked at Henty, releasing his grip on his desk. At least I wasn't alone.

He saw me looking. "We're still running yours. The computer seems to like the letters."

Thaler looked at me. Her well-shaped eyebrows were a shade darker than her hair, which needed only a light rinse to be blond. Not many would resist the temptation the way she had all these years.

"Alvinus C. Adams," I said. "The *C* is for clandestine; another caller after the reward. Day laborer, not laboring anywhere at the moment, not for lack of trying. He was walking his dog past Gates's house when he saw a car loitering suspiciously at the curb. When the driver spotted him, he flipped down his visor, covering his face, and drove off. He got V-A-L off the plate."

"Talk to Adams before Carol Thompson or after?"

"After."

"And you reported this right away?"

"Not right away. He was on the scene the

night before New Year's Eve. It was possible he was casing the place, but it wasn't enough to jump on."

"Half our calls involve strange cars in the neighborhood," Henty said. "Way less than half of them amount to anything. People get lost, pull over to check maps, bang on the GPS. They're early for an appointment, they stop to burn a butt and kill time. A local buys a second car without consulting the neighbors. This time of year it's a visitor warming his motor up more often than not. But we follow them all up. It's not a priority without proper cause."

"I know. I didn't say I was an ex-cop just to impress you. Before I leave, can I have a printout on what you've dug up on those V-A-Ls? It won't come to anything. Life's not *Law and Order.* But you know how the brass thinks."

He smiled his granite smile. "I like how you always ask without using the *W* word. What about your end?"

"I can't promise anything without clearance. If we turn anything that weighs out as common homicide, I'll share." She put away her wonder toy in the handbag where she kept her hideout piece. "I have one more favor to ask: Five minutes with Walker; just us two."

"Aw. Can't I watch?" He got up, grinning. "I'll get that printout."

Alone with me, Mary Ann Thaler unbuttoned her coat and crossed her legs. I couldn't tell if she wore pantyhose or stockings or just tanning lotion, but her legs hadn't suffered from sitting behind a desk in the McNamara Building.

"Place bugged?" she asked.

"It used to be, but Ray Henty doesn't work that way."

"Known him long?"

"How long do you have to know a cop before he shows his tusks?"

"Not long, as I recall." She shrugged one of her square shoulders. I remembered they went with an elegant collarbone, a feature I always looked for in a dress cut low enough. You can't fake that. "Since when do you do gruntwork for the police?"

"I wonder how long it will be," I said.

"Again?"

I was looking at one of the beige walls. "Before the old undercoat wears through. Ever hear of Lucky Strike Green?"

"It sounds before my time."

"Before most people's, mine too. Luckies used to come in a green package, but when the Second World War came along, the company donated the dye to the army for uniforms. They got some publicity mileage out of it, running ads in all the magazines showing a pack of cigarettes marching with a tin hat and a rifle: 'Lucky Strike Green Goes to War.' "

"The advertising business hasn't grown up much since."

"When the war ended, the government was stuck with thousands of gallons of green dye; which is why most official construction during peacetime wound up painted that tough ugly green. You can paint over it, but sooner or later — well." I took my turn at a shrug.

"And your point?"

"I wonder how long it will be before the old ugly Iroquois Heights works its way through the new improved one."

"You didn't answer my question."

"Who's asking, you or Washington?"

"I could find out."

"That answers *my* question. You wouldn't be considering me for a job in the public sector, would you, Deputy? I've been screened before. My jail record's a problem."

"No. I don't have the clearance to requisition paper clips, let alone recruit staff. If you're hard enough up to cold-call cranks, either the local clientele has cleaned up its act or you fucked up big-time.

"I live in town," she went on. "I'm not one of those media cheerleaders who put down their pompons at the end of their shift and go home to their gated communities in the 'burbs. The local clientele wouldn't clean out its trunk, let alone its act. Booze?"

"Yes."

"Drugs?"

"Yes."

The eyebrows lifted.

"Pills," I said. "I got on them to forget that slug that went through my leg, then forgot just why I got on them in the first place. I got off them, but they're like that green paint."

"What about now?"

I knocked on the wood of the desk.

"I'm not asking out of concern," she said. "I need to know if my informants are reliable."

"So I am being screened."

"Not for a job. For the privilege of serving your Uncle Sam."

"I served him when it counted. He never calls, he doesn't write."

"You're refusing?"

"I'm moonlighting as it is. Someone else has hired me to find out who killed Donald Gates and why."

"Does Henty know?"

"No, and I'd like to keep it that way for a while. If he gets wind, he might cut off my pipeline to the investigation."

"You *are* hard up for money, aren't you?"

"Not really. I'm like that horse whose owner fed him one less oat per day until he was living on air. I think Amelie Gates and her son would sleep better at night if they know why they're shy a husband and father."

She shook her head. "I forgot what a sentimental slob you are."

I got out a cigarette and hung it on my lip. I couldn't get away with smoking in that office, but it filled the permanent groove and kept me from leaking oxygen. "See if you still think that when I tell you what I want in return for being your snitch."

Twelve

"No can do," she said. "Letting a civilian in on a federal investigation is the kind of decision I don't get to make."

"You can at least tell me what you're doing."

"You first. Tell me about this Alvinus Adams."

"He looks like he ran into his share of the backs of trains. That could be why he's still looking for work. The dog he was walking is a Chow, he said. It may be a Chinese agent, but they're our creditors now. I gave him a tip on a security job in the old City-County Building in Detroit."

"Stop it. You're killing me with all this altruism."

"I'm only telling you where he might be found when he isn't at home, so you can ring him with angels. If Thompson isn't a coincidence, someone's striking witnesses off the list."

"We'll do what we can — provided he cooperates. Another thing I'm not authorized to do is hand out rewards for information. Making it a crime to lie to a federal officer is one of those little cost-saving measures you people who care so much about the taxpayers like so much."

"I didn't know the First Amendment's written on soap."

"Write your congressman. Stop changing the subject."

"That's fair. I can point a man to safety. Whether he goes there is up to him. What's first on the Yako case?"

"We'll get a warrant to access his computers at home and at work, if we don't get permission from those who can give it. Yako used to earn his keep fencing prescription drugs. We can wash these characters in the blood of the lamb, but we can't change their basic chemistry. They have an annoying habit of getting dirty all over again. If he's been dealing here, we'll know where to start looking for his killer."

"You'll have a hard time hanging it on him without a corpse."

"All we need is to show that mattress to a judge."

"If Lieutenant Henty lets you take it."

"After I intercepted that radio call I got

my section chief out of a meeting. Henty's phone will be ringing any time. Yako was the property of the U.S. government. That takes his murder off local hands."

"You'd think he'd be happy."

"You would, wouldn't you?" She smiled. "It happened to me a couple of times when I was with the DPD. I'm still just so grateful I could spit."

I looked at the picture in the frame on Henty's desk. It had changed: It was one of those electronic jobs that can't make up their mind. Now he was shooting hoops with a much younger version of himself wearing a Michigan State sweatshirt; proof even cops breed in captivity.

"Can I at least ask you to let me know if Yako's death turns out not to be connected with Gates's?" I asked.

"I think so. No details, mind."

"In exchange for all the details I have."

"I didn't think I had to say it."

"You feds. It's like snagging a kite in a tree. The guy throws a tennis ball at it to knock it down and it keeps the tennis ball. Then he throws his racquet at it and it keeps that."

"So buy a new kite."

"*I'm* the kite."

She laughed. Then she lifted her brows.

" *'Suis generis,'* seriously?"

"I've been spending a lot of time in doctors' waiting rooms lately. The reading material's limited."

Henty came in holding a sheaf of paper. "If you gals are through gabbing, I've got news."

Thaler's eyes were better than mine. She'd worn glasses for years, but modern medical science had taken care of that. "Plate numbers? Looks like half the state."

"Like I said, computer's got a hard-on for V-A-L. Begging your pardon, Deputy."

"It's okay. I'm not sure I'd recognize one if I saw it. How many man hours are we looking at?"

He sat behind his desk and slid out a pair of readers. "We got a hundred sixty-three hits on V-A-L; but it isn't as bad as all that. The computer narrowed it down to ninety-two issued in counties in southeastern Michigan. We got some blanks — limo outfits and law enforcement organizations reserve them in blocks, to speed up registration — so we eliminated those. On a hunch I had the geek punch in local rental agencies. Forty-six hits there."

"Decent hunch," Thaler said. "If these were pro jobs, the driver wouldn't be likely to use his own wheels. I've got a way to pare it down further."

"This is my job, not a hobby."

"So sorry."

"I'm sure." He peeled aside a page and looked at the next. "Cars recently reported stolen bearing that partial: none."

"Back to the rental agencies," the deputy said.

"Don't sound so glum. They keep good records."

I said, "What about stolen plates?"

"Nothing applicable so far," Henty said. "Which means nothing. How often does a driver look at his plate? He could go on for weeks until he noticed it missing while he was washing his car or a cop pulled him over. It's snow-and-slush season, so even a sharp-eyed prowlie might not spot it. Then, more than likely, when asked the number, the owner doesn't have it memorized and has to dig out his registration and look it up. Pair that with the fact he's reporting to the Secretary of State's office and not the police, factor in the hang time before it's reported to us — *if* it's reported; we're talking civil service here —"

"Stop. I can always look at my date book when I feel like being depressed." Thaler finished entering data into her thingamajig. "Which leaves us just as out in the cold as when we started. We know the car that was used in the hit-and-run was either an Olds Alero, made the year GM dropped the Oldsmobile division, or maybe a Honda Civic — 'blue or gray in color,' the report says, as if it could be blue or gray in anything else. It'll have front-end damage and no doubt DNA on the undercarriage, but without a registration we can't start looking for it until we actually find it. If he's our man V-A-L, and he stole the plate, he could just as easily swipe another."

The lieutenant tossed the printout onto his desk. "License registration is like a lock. It only keeps honest people honest."

I got up.

Thaler looked up at me. "Where are you going?"

"I just remembered two things. I'm not in the car-finding business, and I'm not under arrest."

"That's no answer," she said.

"I signed on to help find out who killed Donald Gates. Maybe it was Yako, maybe somebody wanted us to think it was Yako, and patched a pothole with Thompson to make it stick. I'm going to check out Gates's hunting buddies. If anyone knows anyone else, he learned it living under the same roof for at least a week."

"And if they can't tell you anything?" Henty said.

"Then I'm going to find out how many of them are heeled enough to have put up the reward for his killer's conviction."

He took off his glasses. "I've been a cop longer than I wasn't. I never saw a dipsy-doodle alibi like that stand up longer than a soap bubble."

Thaler said, "Let him try to pop it. Maybe it'll keep him out of the way while us grown-ups work."

"Giving orders, Deputy?" asked Henty.

"Call it assisting," I cut in. "It's friendlier."

The rain had subtracted itself from the equation, and finally we were getting snow: those hard tiny urban kernels that all look alike no matter what you hear, cling to the wipers in pale strands like freshwater pearls, and whipsnake across the pavement driven by the wind. I saw parkas, hoodies, camo, and the occasional case of denial in T-shirt and flip-flops plunging across the street without looking either direction and walking backwards into the teeth of the mini-blizzard. Pigeons perched on ledges were puffed up like stuffed squab.

The official groundhog in Pennsylvania had seen his shadow, auguring six more weeks of winter. His competitor in rural Livingston County had missed his, predicting early spring. For a while it seemed a third expert in Wisconsin had broken the tie, but he turned out to be a muskrat and was disenfranchised.

The season would grind on regardless, broken up by the thaws that seem exclusive to Michigan, that have you cranking down the air conditioner and cranking up the furnace in the same twelve-hour period. The climate's been changing like that since before mastodons wandered down Woodward Avenue.

Meanwhile everyone in the frozen world was learning how to drive all over again. Five cars passed me on the right driving ten over the limit, and a minivan straddled the now-you-see-it-now-you-don't white line going slow enough to pass for reverse. A gull-wing yellow sports job whipped out of a side street, taking three lines in a sliding loop, and wound up facing west in the eastbound, two car lengths in front of me. I started moving again and pulled around it. I needed a wrecking bar to uncramp my fingers from the wheel.

My cell rang. I pulled over to take the call, my heart still throbbing in my throat. The number, which I didn't recognize, turned out to belong to the tough little blonde in the rehab center in Highland Park.

"Have you made an appointment yet with that therapist?"

"One moment, Doctor." I laid the cell on the passenger's seat, plucked a cigarette out of the pack with my teeth, and spent a couple of matches getting it lit. I drew the smoke in deep, let it stagger out, and picked up the phone.

"I was just about to place the call," I said.

"I recommend it. I meant what I said about turning you over to the authorities."

"Are you calling me over a real phone or that runty laptop?"

"What difference does it make?"

"I'd hate to have you ruin those blue eyes staring at a screen. I'll make the call today." I gave the cheap cell a shake, which always made it crackle, and ended the call. People almost never do anything when they think it was dropped. They wait for you to call back. In light of that I'm prepared to let technology go on a little longer.

THIRTEEN

Amelie Gates frowned at her cards. "What's a bower again? I'm sorry."

"Don't be. I had to bone up on the game myself before coming here." I explained it, dealing a couple of hands to imaginary players. Playing euchre was like opening the cedar chest where my mother packed the hunting clothes: The smell of mothballs and evergreen and the motion of slapping a card down faceup took me back to a three-room cabin in Grayling that was out in the woods then but the last time I drove past it was well inside the city limits. The oil pig was missing, also the outhouse in back. What sort of people lived there now I couldn't guess.

"Impatience was one of Don's few faults. Every card game he tried to teach me wound up in a fight."

"A good game of euchre sounds like one. My father was a Teamster. When I was five,

I heard Jimmy Hoffa swearing in the kitchen. I thought he was killing my dad, but it turned out they were just playing cards. You can't really play it properly without a little blasphemy."

"Wasn't Jimmy Hoffa some kind of gangster?"

"No."

We were sitting in a combined kitchen and dining room in her house in Iroquois Heights, at a round oak table in a bay window. The place was spotless, as widows' houses often are. It had stopped snowing. A car swept down the street, churning slush, and stopped for a light with a long slurring noise of warm rubber on slick asphalt. A cube pushed itself out of the ice maker in the refrigerator and landed with a clunk. It was one of those days peculiar to a Michigan winter, when you could hear a spider pat back a yawn in its web and watch a drowsy fly drift past. Now and then a hole opened in the overcast, drenching us both in warm sunlight, swirling with motes that glittered like gold dust as they turned. We were like two housecats napping with a bellyful of tuna.

She watched me arrange the two cards at my elbow. "Why don't you keep score on a piece of paper, like in cribbage?"

"No reason. It's just the way I was taught." I moved the card I'd placed facedown on top of the nine of clubs, exposing two of the pips. "That's two for me and one for you. I'm being hustled."

"You're sweet." She drew a card from her hand slowly, biting her lower lip and looking to me for guidance. I nodded. She played it. In about twenty minutes she was beating the pants off me. It's that kind of game.

"Oh, I have those names for you. Don's old hunting buddies. I'm not sure if the addresses and telephone numbers are still good. It's been years."

"The names will help. I know someone who knows how to use a computer. He should be able to track them down if they're still breathing." I played a six of hearts.

"You don't use one?"

"I try not to have appliances in my house that are smarter than me."

"The world's passing you by."

"It keeps turning. I'll catch it on the next pass, or the one after that."

"I like this game. It's reassuring, somehow."

"Sure. You can't play it without going by the rules."

"Is that some kind of philosophy?"

"It's just a game. Don't make it out to be anything more than it is."

She rearranged the cards in her hand. "Should we be doing this?"

"We haven't even made a bet. Anyway I'm tight with the sheriff."

"Not that. What would Don think? Gone just six weeks, and here I am —"

She broke down then.

"Your play," I said.

She swept the back of her hand across her eyes, sniffed, nodded, and laid down a six of hearts.

"It's not just that," she said. "I'm keeping you from your investigation."

"Yeah. I'm that lazy." I drew a three of clubs; no help there. "I'm here because I promised, but I could've done that anytime. There's someone I want to talk to."

"Who?"

Fate's a good stage manager. Just then a door banged and noise shot through the house like thudding thunder or a helicopter flying low over the roof: seventy pounds of boy in blue jeans, clodhopper sneakers, and a lumpy Michelin Man parka, dumping a backpack on a table, a pair of mittens on the floor six feet apart, and a brown knitted watch cap that hovered in midair like a chimney cinder before it fell in a crumple to the rug, the rest of it streaking past us in a red-blue blur. All that was missing was the "beep-beep."

"Michel! Slow down! We have company."

The boy skidded to a halt, staring at me with his mother's black-olive eyes in his father's generic face. "Sorry."

"Don't be," I said. "Just leave some of that for me."

"Some of what?"

"Don't be rude. This is Mr. Walker. He's the man I told you about."

He looked at me more steadily, a thin boy — a growth spurt caught in stop-motion — every follicle of his black hair fighting training. His energy had flattened into a quiet idle. "The man who's going to find out who killed my father?"

"Do you want me to?"

"I guess." He went into another room and shut the door.

I don't know why I'd asked; or for that matter why I wasn't surprised by the answer.

FOURTEEN

She started to get up. I waved her back down with my hand of cards. "I'm an expert on kids, never having had any. Give him a chance to wind down before you stir him up."

She hesitated, then subsided into her seat. "He's not usually like that. Well, he was, before the school nurse prescribed Ritalin. Even then it was a long time before he settled down. But for a week now he's been more like a normal boy."

"I'd like to talk to him, but not now. Maybe sometime when the slow-down juice kicks in."

Her eyes were big. "Michel's the one you meant? What could he tell you? He was sleeping at the babysitter's house the night —"

"Where was he the day before?"

"At home; it was Christmas vacation. But so was I. What's the day before got to do with anything?"

"Could be nothing. Someone saw a driver behaving strangely in front of this house that day. It might be nothing, but of two other witnesses I've spoken with, one's dead and the other went missing, but not before he left behind a lot of blood."

She put down her cards.

"When were you going to tell me this?"

"I wasn't. Officially I shouldn't have now; the cops get territorial when there's a stiff involved. Between us, knowing it wouldn't have done you any good. Not until either the cops or I find the holes the loose bricks fit into. This game's one for the cat." I threw in my hand and stood. "Can I have that list?"

She rose, opened a drawer in a maple secretary, and handed me a sheet of bright pink paper with a smiling yellow sun in one corner. She had a round, schoolgirl hand and dotted her eyes with circles. I forgave her for that, seeing as how she was so good at euchre.

I started local. The owner of the third name on the list had an office in Centerline, in a sprawling new redbrick building on a four-lane highway where the commuters played Grand Theft Auto with real cars. I sat in the turning lane two minutes before I caught a break, then had to gun it to avoid the driver of a low-slung yellow pickup who tried to close the gap with a spurt. The marks of my tires are still on the asphalt, probably.

A short hallway leading from the entrance made a T in the center. I eenie-meenied my way left, past three empty-looking smoked-glass offices to one in the corner, with a silver-etched sign on the glass reading:

RICHARD PERLBERG, P.C.

The door closed itself behind me, making as much noise as a cat yawning on a sunny sill, and I found myself in another shallow passage containing four chromium-and-black-leather chairs and a pile of swanky magazines on a glass table, with a receptionist's nook at the cross of another T at the end. It was going unused at the moment.

I had an appointment, but I was five minutes early. I took a seat and opened a copy of *Hour,* a Detroit publication about the size of a plat book, with glossy pages and not much print to clutter up the photos. There was nothing in them I recognized; it publishes in the suburbs, with a well-dressed security man at the door.

"Mr. Walker?" A smiling middle-aged

woman stood in front of the receptionist's desk with her hands folded at her waist. She'd come in as quietly as the door closed. I was some detective that day.

I put aside the article I was reading about a sushi restaurant I'd never heard of and got up.

"Mr. Perlberg's ready for you. Just down that hall."

"Dandy."

Another left turn brought me to a large square office with the door propped open. A young balding man got up from behind a glass-topped desk supporting a multiline telephone, an electronic calculator, and an electric stapler. Printed forms made orderly stacks on a credenza behind his chair. The outfit specialized in opening tax loopholes for small businesses.

"Quite a spread you have here, Mr. Perlberg." I sat down in a comfy chair facing the desk.

"Richard, please. We try to put people at ease." Squidging up his nose, he tilted back in his swivel and propped an argyle-clad foot on the desk. "Thanks for the compliment. I own the whole shebang, and Peggy and I are the only souls in it. I built it just before the wonks in Washington lowered mortgage rates straight into the second

Great Depression. We're offering the first three months free to anyone who'll sign a year's lease. You saw how many takers we've had on your way down the hall."

"How long can you hold out?"

He cleared his throat, straightened his tie — silver, to match the lettering on the glass outside — and sat up, wriggling his foot into an unseen shoe. "I don't mean to be unsociable, but I'm swamped this time of year. No time for small talk. I'd've put you off when you called until after April fifteenth, but since it's about Don, I can give you five minutes."

"That's okay. I really don't give a damn about the rest. You used to hunt with Gates in Canada. Did he have any enemies his wife doesn't know about?"

"Jesus, no. Kind of hunter he was, even the elk didn't have anything against him. Is that all you wanted to know? You could've asked over the phone."

"I've got four and a half minutes coming. Anything about him didn't seem to fit the rest of him?"

"I'm not sure I understand the question."

"A bunch of men shut up together get to know each other, sometimes better than their wives: no guards, no games. Amelie helped her father run the hunting lodge.

You were there when they were becoming close. Did he act or say something you wouldn't have expected of him, knowing him as well as you did?"

He smiled.

"Who doesn't, man? Who doesn't, when the love bug bites?"

"How about later, after they were married and before he dropped out of the group?"

"Can't help you there. He only made one trip after the wedding, and I wasn't there. One of my clients was being audited, an important one. It was my rep on the line."

"I got this from his wife." I snapped open the pink sheet and laid it on his desk. "Rule out any who weren't present that last trip."

"Oh, they were all there. Rudy Johnson brought down a buck ran close to eight hundred pounds; could've been a moose if it didn't watch its carbs. Amelie's father took their picture with it. The guys are still ribbing me about not being there. Here." He swiveled, stretched an arm, scooped a standing frame off the credenza, and poked it at me.

It was a collector's item: a Polaroid, with a greenish cast. Six men in checked flannel shirts, baggy woolen pants, and three-day beards with an eighteen-point monster hanging on an outdoor pole between them, towering evergreens in the background. Donald Gates stood at one end. He was the one who wasn't smiling.

Which meant exactly nothing. Maybe the only time he'd ever grinned for the camera was when he was caught off-guard at Christmas.

"Gates's eyes look red. Did he drink heavily on these trips?"

"Don? Hell, no. Beer now and then, just to fit in. You could get drunk off the dregs he left in the bottle. Rudy was the drinker in that crowd. I bet he polished off two six-packs a day. He must've been aiming at something else when he hit that buck."

"His name's not on the list."

"No reason it should be. His liver gave up on him a couple of years ago. His wife and kids gave up on him a long time before that."

I looked closer. It could have been ordinary flashbulb red-eye. The more I looked the more I was sure of it.

"Any of these guys closer to Gates than the others?"

"Well, Rudy, if you know what I mean. He was a huggy drunk, one of those 'I love you, guys' guys. I guess his folks never told him they loved him."

"I mean still putting out carbon dioxide."

For a man with only five minutes to spare, he was hard to reel in.

"That'd be Chuck." He pointed at a man standing next to Gates, close to his age and dusky, with whiskers blacker than the rest, to match his hair. "Chuck Swingline. He's a half-blood Ojibway, the leader of our gang and the best hunter in three counties. He took Don under his wing the first day he showed up at the lodge; you know, giving him the benefit of Indian ways. Not that he ever gained anything by them, but Chuck never gave up. Between you and me?" Perlberg leaned forward, resting his forearms on the desk. "I think he had a man-crush, Chuck did, not that he ever did anything about it, I'm sure of that. You could chop wood using his chin for a block. But if there was anything ginchy going on with Don that last trip, he's your man."

Charles Swingline's name was fourth on the list, with an address in Ottawa, Canada.

I had just the fellow for that job. I thanked Perlberg and left him to his empty building.

"Loyal Dominion, Toronto office."

The woman sounded like a cheerleader her first day on a part-time job. I remembered a plastic hairband and a charm bracelet that made as much racket as a bucket of coins falling down a metal staircase.

"Amos Walker for Llewellyn Hale."

"Oh, yes, Mr. Walker. I remember you. One moment."

I listened to Anne Murray singing "Snowbird" for thirty seconds. I wondered if they laid on the Canada so thick when someone local called.

"Amos? You in the country?"

The quasi-British accent was still there, callow-sounding coming from a youthful body connected to a brain as old as Solomon's and almost as sharp. He'd helped me crack two homicides spaced a half-century apart, at the expense of adding two more to the score.

"Why? I don't play outdoor hockey. I've got a job for you up at the capital."

"Shoot."

I gave him the particulars. Keys rattled on his end.

"It shouldn't take long," I said. "Your day rate should cover it, plus travel."

"No travel. I've got a branch up there now. But getting those Ojibway to open up can be like cracking a bowling ball with your toe. My guy there's French-Canadian. That's better than American, and way better than British where they're concerned.

Pontiac's Conspiracy might have wrapped up just last week."

"I don't guess it's kosher to tell him to bring along some beads."

"I'm not sure whether that remark is anti-Indian or anti-Semitic."

"Hogwash. I'm part English, German, Jewish, French, Serbian, Croatian, and Italian, and my ex-wife was one-sixteenth Cherokee. I'm bulletproof."

He said he'd be in touch and we ended the conversation.

I had three names left on the list, one in Grand Rapids, the other in Toledo. The convenient address was on Evergreen just north of Outer Drive.

A wife answered the telephone. When I told her my errand she clucked sympathetically and said her husband was at work, but would be home around six. I looked at my watch. Four o'clock. I said I'd be there and got off the line.

I paid a bill and tore up a couple of second notices, but it didn't take up near enough time as I'd hoped. The place was in Redford Township, where the therapist I was supposed to see kept her office.

I blew out air and called the number I had in my notebook. A foggy-voiced receptionist told me I was in luck: There'd been a cancellation, and could I be there in an hour? I couldn't catch a break.

Fifteen

The cell rang while I was crossing Eight Mile Road. It was Ray Henty.

"What part of 'Stay away from the wife' didn't you understand?" he said by way of greeting.

"Who ratted?"

"The wife. She called the substation to ask if we'd turned anything and said you'd just left. It's coming up on four forty-five. I'm going to play Santa Claus and throw in the extra fifteen so you can draw your salary for another full day. Apart from that consider yourself canned as of this moment."

"Don't play dumb, Lieutenant. The job was over when I gave you what I got from those anonymous callers, but you didn't give me my time, so I figured I was still a junior deputy. Who does anyone go to when a married man is killed?"

"If it gets out I hired a civilian to do my

job, I won't even be a junior. You're interfering in an official investigation."

"I'm just covering ground you already did." I told him where I was headed, leaving out the side trip to see the shrink.

"We already checked those guys. They're clean, and none of them's had any contact with Gates in years. Their phone records checked with that. Now you're just wasting public money."

"You said 'wasting.' That mean I'm still on the payroll?"

"Yes, goddamn it. When I start to fuck things up, it's best to go ahead and finish the job."

"You should put that on a sampler. Anything new?"

"Deputy Thaler's a good egg when it comes to cooperating with local law. She can't last long. That computer Yako was using lit up every illegal drug Web site in both hemispheres. Looks like he was ordering and dealing; which may mean his death, if he had one, had nothing to do with Gates. Don't you just love it when a case splits in two?"

The therapist's name was Miernik, and right away I hated her for being too easy to like. She asked me to call her Jeannie.

"As in 'meany,' " she said, "but not 'weenie,' and I'm just tall enough to resent 'teenie.' "

She looked just enough like the sturdy blond doctor in Highland Park I suspected nepotism in the recommendation, but she was not so much a walking fist. She was tall enough, and more; our eyes were on a level when she shook my hand at the door from the receptionist's office. She had gray eyes with green flecks in them and chestnut hair cut short and teased into curls around the border of her face; which normally to hell with it, but her face didn't seem to have been made for any other style. No-nonsense flats, a tan skirt, and a tailored hip-length sweater over a black top was her working uniform. I tagged her for a well-put-up forty.

The office was furnished straight from the Property Department: wood-print desk, documents on the walls, a pot full of Spanish bayonet, chairs and a sofa covered with green Naugahyde. It was attached to a private house with a child's-size sled on the front lawn. "Okay if I sit?" I asked. "I fall asleep in five minutes stretched out on a couch."

"Of course. I only tolerate the damn thing because one of my first patients was disappointed I didn't have one. If I were a mechanic, I suppose I'd have to wear one of those crowns made from a felt hat and hang up a girlie calendar. I hate that plant," she said, scowling at the pot. "I haven't watered it in a month, but it won't die, just to spite me."

We sat facing each other in the conversation area. She held up a tape recorder that looked like an oversize Pez dispenser. "Okay? I find it easier to concentrate when I'm not taking notes."

"Sure. Just don't play it back when I'm around. I like to think I sound like Gregory Peck."

She turned it on and set it on a marble-topped coffee table.

"Is this a nonsmoking office?" I asked.

"The law says so, but ignoring it often saves me a whole session putting people at ease."

She got up, fetched a glass ashtray from a desk drawer, switched on a doohickey the size of a camp refrigerator on the floor near the window, and sat down while it was whirring, sliding the ashtray across the table. I lit up. The smoke made a beeline for the air filter or whatever it was.

"The doctor in rehab sent me your file," she said. "I had time to go over it before the appointment. Are you really a private detective?"

"Why would I lie?"

"Do you carry a gun?"

"I tolerate it for my clients. If I were a therapist I'd have to have a couch in my office. No plant, though; the city keeps hiking the water rates."

"You quit Vicodin. Why'd you go back?"

I told her about the dead little girl in the sex offender's house. She listened with a poker face, but her eyes flicked toward the sled outside.

"Of course that was just an excuse," she said. "Better than most, but you can admit you were looking for one."

"I was looking for a little girl."

"What are you working on now?"

"A homicide."

"Now that's two that I know about. I didn't think private investigators got involved with that kind of case."

"It has a way of involving me more often than I like."

"Did you ever think of turning it down? Stress plays the biggest part in re-addiction."

"Every time. But starving to death is stressful too."

"There are other jobs."

"Not at my age, and not with my résumé."

"Can you discuss the case?"

"I can, but I won't."

"Confidentiality?"

"Not this time. It's on billboards all over three counties. But once I start talking about an investigation it takes all the wind out of my sails. I can't afford to sleepwalk my way through a job with a corpse in the equation. Murder's contagious."

"I never thought of it that way."

"No reason you should. On my side, there's no reason I should ask complete strangers if they hated their mothers."

"That's a hoary old cliché. I'm a Jungian, not a Freudian."

I filed that away in my collective unconscious.

"In Highland Park you said you got addicted the first time after you were shot. What happened?"

"A client's husband mistook me for a deer. Then he mistook himself."

"You're starting to sound like one of those private eyes on television."

"I wish I were. Those TV dicks shake off lead like dandruff."

She was quiet for a minute, during which the recorder made no sound at all. I figured it had a chip instead of reels. I was starting to feel like a wart on a dinosaur's tail.

"Your file says you're divorced. How long?"

"Long enough to drop 'divorced' from my self-description."

"Children?"

"No, thank God."

"Why 'thank God'?"

I jerked my thumb in the general direction of the sled in the yard.

"That could have been the trigger you were looking for when that little girl turned up," she said. "Empty-nest syndrome isn't confined to people who raised children."

She was good. It had taken me weeks in rehab to work that one out.

"When was the last time you took a Vicodin or anything similar?"

"Last night."

"You realize you could go to jail for that, after what you were told."

"I had a drink. That's been legal a long time. You said anything similar."

"Now you're just being difficult."

"I'm being shrunk. But you're right. I'm sorry."

"I wasn't asking for an apology. I'm not exactly an amateur when it comes to dealing with people's defense mechanisms."

"You're trying to pour a sidewalk and I'm

walking straight through the cement. No one needs that."

A pair of strong eyebrows got lifted. "Thank you."

"Ask me anything. I loved my mother, by the way."

"Lucky you."

I grinned. I was liking her more and more.

"When was the last time you wanted to take a prescription painkiller?"

"I want to right now."

"Are you always this candid?"

"No. A doctor's office is like the confessional. Why go and then lie your head off?"

"But you're not here under your will."

"I could've fought that; I know more lawyers than most people, and some of them owe me favors. But I didn't think it would hurt, and it might help. At my time of life I don't bounce so well."

"Are you concerned about getting old?"

"A little. Fortunately I'm no good at math."

"Joking is just a way of dealing with what terrifies us."

"If you read my file, you know I started out to be a cop. I still am, in a left-hand way. You're not telling me a thing I didn't already know."

"I didn't intend to. Psychotherapy is nine-tenths common sense."

"What's the other tenth?"

"One hundred thousand dollars in student loans." Her legs were crossed also. She bounced a slim foot in a low-cut cordovan. Then she leaned forward and switched off the recorder.

"I'll have Susan prepare your bill."

"That's it? I'm cured?"

She pursed her lips. "In my profession you learn not to use such words. Plumbers can afford to guarantee their work. I can't. But in my opinion, you're at less risk of re-addiction than some of my esteemed colleagues."

"You'll tell that to the doctor in Highland Park?"

"Not the part about my esteemed colleagues. You might have noticed she's still recovering from a humorectomy."

"You don't have to like someone just because she saved your life, but I'm glad she did."

"You're something different in patients, Mr. Walker. I'm almost sorry to let you go."

I squashed out my cigarette and put a card under the ashtray.

She smiled. She had nice teeth: At sixty dollars an hour she could afford them, with or without the loan payments. "I'm not planning to be part of any murders."

"That's encouraging," I said. "It means you're bound to get hungry sometime. I just read about a new sushi place in *Hour* magazine. Where do you stand on raw fish?"

She smiled. "And you claim to be a detective. You saw that sled in the yard."

"It's what I didn't see that made me ask."

She glanced down at her ringless left hand. She folded her right on top of it.

"Divorce is a hazard of the profession, like cops and lawyers. I like my food cooked, thank you; especially this far from any ocean." She unfolded her hands, picked up my card, and slid it down inside her top.

Sixteen

Walter Cole led me into his den in a house built of golden logs, a comfortable room paneled in cedar with a row of scoped rifles in a glazed lock rack and the mounted heads of an elk, a couple of whitetail, a mule deer, and something brown with white fur at the throat and a pair of horns as long and straight as knitting needles. I think it was some kind of African jackalope. We sat in deep leather armchairs and sipped twelve-year-old Scotch from barrel glasses belonging to a fully stocked bar made out of a wine cask. The place smelled of good cigars and single malt and looked like Clyde Beatty threw up.

Cole himself was a lean fifty or so with square shoulders, a narrow waist, and a thick mat of hair in the V of his open-necked shirt. He had a full head of brown hair with gray splinters and wore glasses with black rims.

"You'll have to speak up a little," he said. "If I'd known about ear protection when I was fourteen, I wouldn't be so deaf."

I raised my voice. We talked about this and that, compared hunting stories; people with a hearing disability take time to draw out. When he was in a conversational mood I switched gears.

"Richard Perlberg says Rudy Johnson was the best hunter in the outfit. It looks like he had competition."

"Had; even when he was still with us." He adjusted his eyeglasses. "Ever hunt elk?"

"Just deer."

"Deer can be quiet when they sense danger, walk through dry leaves knee-deep and make no more noise than an ant farting in a box of cotton. Elk don't bother. They think they're indestructible, especially the bulls. They walk loud, they breathe loud, they shake their ears and you'd swear it's a seven-forty-seven taking off. When you get so you can't hear an elk, your hunting days are through." He glanced around the room. "I think I'll donate all this stuff to the Fred Bear Museum and hang paintings. I can't look at them anymore. It's like a has-been athlete looking at a picture of himself when he could still fit into the uniform."

"Paintings are nice. I like clowns and kids

with big cow eyes."

"I dream about that lodge up in Canada," he said, drinking. "In the dream, I'm in the woods, and when I realize I left my rifle behind I go back for it, but the door's locked and I've lost the key. What do you think that means?"

"There's a doctor right in this neighborhood you can ask. How well did you know Don Gates?"

"Better than most. You know what they say about hunting camps?"

"It's true. He looked a little threadbare in the last picture he posed for with you and the rest. Did he seem different from other times?"

"Quieter than usual, I thought; and he was a quiet guy. But I wasn't really in the game. I was going through my third divorce at the time. She turned vegan just to spite me."

"I can't find anyone who'll say anything against Gates."

"Being dead will do that. But if that's what you're looking for, I'd talk to Chuck Swingline."

"Perlberg said they were close."

"He said that?"

There are times when I like the work; one of them is when sources clash. I let the bobber ride and waited for the strike.

A square shoulder rose, fell. "Well, maybe he saw something I didn't. That miserable Indian didn't open his mouth more than six times in six years, and then it was to tell us what rotten hunters we white men were. The more time you spent with him, the more you understood Custer. We'd have dropped him after the first year if he didn't have such a talent for finding the best spots. Call me a racist if you like, but they're born with it."

"I wonder where Perlberg got the impression he and Gates liked each other."

"Who knows? Those handlebucks don't think like the rest of us."

"No love lost there, I guess."

"Don't make anything out of that. So long as a guy kicks into the kitty for smokes and bacon, he's good for another season. We didn't have anything in common apart from that and a taste for venison. At least that's one thing I haven't lost. You?"

"It was my first solid food." I took a sip of the smoky stuff in my glass. "Did Gates ever talk about his family?"

"Now that you mention it, he did say something funny about it that last trip. He wasn't the type to make jokes about wives and kids; he'd laugh when one of us did, but he didn't join in. Well, I asked him how

Amelie was — we were there, you know, when they fell for each other — and he said she's a wonderful mother."

"What's strange about that?"

"It was the way he said it." He hesitated, tipped up his glass, but he didn't drink right away, just spoke into it, as if to hear the echo. "I'm hard of hearing, remember. Probably I imagined it. But to me it sounded like he envied her."

It was dark when I left. Snow fell in flakes too small to see, touching my face when I was unlocking the Cutlass and then the windshield in the backwash from my headlights, starring like pebble-cracks when they touched glass. The wind was picking up and the air smelled of iron oxide. A storm was predicted, complete with cub reporters doing breathless stand-ups in front of traffic whizzing along the highway at sixty. The plows were out, but they were parked, with the operators drumming their hands on the wheels, blowing smoke out the windows and counting the hours in dollars.

While I was waiting for the defogger to warm up, I called Amelie Gates to ask if Michel was in a mood where I could talk to him, but her line was busy. Then I tried Mary Ann Thaler's cell to ask about the drug activity the marshals had found on Yuri Yako's computer. It went straight to voice mail. I didn't leave a message. Everybody was sure busy for an hour after quitting time.

I turned down the blower and switched on the radio just as the local news was coming on. Then I forgot all about the calls.

It was a two-bagger: The police in Royal Oak had found Yako's body, and the Detroit cops were questioning a person of interest in the hit-and-run killing of Roy Thompson, the man who'd heard the Ukrainian as much as threaten Donald Gates's life.

Seventeen

Royal Oak was closer, but I didn't know anyone with that department, and anyway most metropolitan area homicide squads conferred with Detroit.

John Alderdyce was in the break room at the Third Precinct, which was filling in for headquarters while Animal Control smoked the critters out of the spongy walls at 1300 Beaubien and the mayor found the money to fix the floor. The inspector was the biggest thing in the room apart from the full-size refrigerator; a slab of black granite in more casual attire than I'd ever seen him in at work, a navy sweatshirt with the police officers' union coat-of-arms on the front, faded jeans, and high-topped Nikes.

"Is it Friday?" I shook his calloused mitt.

"It was either this or my Scooby-Doo pajamas. I pulled three shifts back-to-back, one on furlough. I just hit the sheets when the phone rang. It was your friend Henty, who heard about it when everyone else did. I'm still not clear on why h-and-r gets someone in my pay scale out of bed."

I didn't ask where Henty was. I stalled on the picture of Alderdyce in Scooby-Doo pajamas.

The toaster on the counter shot a strawberry Pop-Tart into his hand; he had the reflexes of a bonus baby. "Haven't had lunch since breakfast," he said with his mouth full, "and come to think of it I didn't have breakfast. We're letting our boy steep a bit in Interview Room A, come up with a flimsy enough excuse for the gray matter on his busted grille to break him."

"Is it an Alero or a Honda?"

"Kia. In my nightmares I'm run over by a foreign job in the middle of Woodward and it shows up in my obituary. What do you know about it?"

"It's connected to the Gates murder in Iroquois Heights. You heard about that."

"Since before his church decided to make him a celebrity. We shook loose some of our own for the early legwork. What's your end?"

"Legwork. The sitting-down kind." I told about the anonymous calls, skipping the rest. I had to leave something for the lieutenant.

"So now you're a bounty hunter."

"I gave up on all that about the time I found out about Santa Claus. It's in the way of a paid favor for Ray. Isn't he here?"

"On his way. He had to brief the Lord High Sheriff first." He had a prejudice against elected cops, for some reason.

The door swung and Henty came in. He had on his working clothes: sportcoat, slacks, and loafers, but he'd ditched the necktie. He looked ten years older than when I'd seen him last, but I decided to be kind and blamed the fluorescents. He shook Alderdyce's hand and looked at me. He had cops' eyes, bleak as November and flat as steel slugs.

"I might've known. Why don't I just resign and put you in charge?"

"The money would spoil me."

"Har; and while I'm at it, har. It's a little early for badinage, don't you think?"

"Never, when I can get a cop to lay out three syllables back-to-back." I looked at Alderdyce. "How do we know this is the Thompson hit-and-run? It's always Shark Week in this town."

"First one in a week, according to Motor Vehicle. That has to be some kind of record. Forensics says the tissue's fresh."

Henty ran a hand over his brush cut.

"Name?"

The inspector took a folded sheet of department stationery out of a hip pocket and snapped it open. His Palmer penmanship held up even during the wee hours. "Boris Ataman. What's that, Russian?"

Henty and I answered together. "Ukrainian."

"How the hell do you know that?"

"It's that kind of case," I said.

"Homework, on my part," Henty said. "After Yako went missing I Googled the country, got a shitload of Cossack history. Some of it stuck. 'Ataman' is a ranking officer. Five bucks says if we go back far enough I bet we find at least one captain in a fuzzy hat hanging from his family tree. With what Thaler found on Yako's computer, I'll lay another fin we're dealing with the Ukrainian mob."

Alderdyce brightened. "Thaler as in Mary Ann? You know, I've seen her more often since she went to Washington than when she worked at Thirteen Hundred. How's it I'm just hearing about all this now? Walker's chin's been nailed shut as long as I've known him, but I thought we'd get a little more cooperation from the Heights since it shook out the bozos."

"She just came into it, and the mob theory

was just a hunch based on Yako's background. Two Cossacks on the same case may be a coincidence in Kiev. In Detroit it's evidence."

Alderdyce yawned bitterly.

"Seeing as how you're up on your borscht, I'm going to make you primary in interrogation. Call your sheriff if you need an okay."

"Actually," Henty said, "I need to ask *her.*"

He was facing the door, where Mary Ann Thaler was standing, wearing the same cute hat and fun fur she'd had on the last time I saw her.

Eighteen

"You're dressed for the part," Alderdyce said. "How's the turbulence over the Volga this time of year?"

"Same as here, also the climate. But I'm just back from Royal Oak. Couple of kids found Yako in a condemned house three blocks from the Shrine of the Little Flower, of local legend. They said they were exploring, but one of them has a juvie record for scavenging scrap metal, so you can be sure they were looking for copper pipe." She smiled. "Hello, John. I'm glad to see you stopped wearing neckties. They're bad for the circulation."

"Everybody's got something to say about my sartorial choices. Next time I'll rent a tuxedo."

"What was C.O.D.?" Henty asked Thaler.

"Desanguination: such a pretty word for bleeding to death. Shakespeare could have written a sonnet around it. Four quarts, if I remember my forensics training. The case is still too green to decide whether they used a shotgun or a machete. He's missing his midsection."

"I'd guess a saber," I said. "But I'm a romantic."

"My first question is why they didn't just leave him where they sliced him up."

Henty said, "Maybe we'll know when we have time of death. Maybe he wasn't quite dead when they smuggled him out of his apartment. Nothing there; there's a back stairs for carrying up furniture and carrying down evidence in a felony. They took him someplace, maybe the condemned house, to get what they could out of him before he finished bleeding out."

"He must have had double the usual," she said.

Alderdyce said, "We get more variety in plain Homicide than you did in Felony Murder. I worked a couple of devil-worshipping cases, some dandy dismemberments in bathtubs, a daughter decapitated by her father in Dearborn; she was involved with a gentile, and the old man was an Islamic traditionalist. It looked like someone opened a fire hydrant full of cherry Kool-Aid. Blood always looks like more than it is."

"Like spilled milk," I said. "Somebody didn't want his absence known too soon; that's why they went to all the trouble of flipping the mattress and making the bed."

Thaler took off her floppy hat and rearranged her hair with her fingers.

"Let's ask Boris."

I thought I recognized the furniture on the other side of the two-way glass: Back at 1300 I'd sat in orange scoop chairs at cheap chipboard tables often enough to qualify for a perfect attendance certificate, and the city was too broke to let them go to waste in that rotting building. The man occupying one of the chairs sat tracing someone's initials in the veneer with a blunt forefinger. He was blunt all over, with fair hair mowed close to a broad scalp, a bony promontory overhanging pale eyes, and no more neck than a jar of pickles. He wore a green work suit and a pair of square-toed boots on his big square feet. I'd seen more curves in a Rock 'em Sock 'em Robot.

From the crown of his head, his skull fell straight down the back to his collar. That flattened cerebellum is a common characteristic among some eastern Europeans. All he needed was gold frogs on a scarlet tunic and a bearskin hat to star in a road show version of *Doctor Zhivago.*

So when he finally opened his mouth to spell his name for the record, I was surprised to hear a light baritone with a Midwestern drone and not the deep burring speech of the western steppes.

"What's your address, Mr. Ataman?" Thaler asked.

"Sixteen-forty-two Mound."

"What do you do for a living?"

"Tinsmith at GM in Warren."

"Your hands aren't very calloused for someone who works with tin snips."

"Join the twenty-first, lady. It's all electronic now."

"If you call me anything, call me Deputy. I'm with the U.S. Marshals' office."

Only his lower teeth showed when he smiled. "Your name wouldn't be Dillon, by any chance?"

"The cowboy or the actor? Don't answer. The name's Thaler. Your car was pulled over because it didn't have any plates. Where'd you ditch the V-A-L?"

"I don't know what you mean. That's what this is about, no plates? I thought you feds set your sights higher."

Thaler touched the nosepiece of a pair of glasses she hadn't worn in years.

"You ran down a man named Thompson

the other night; the officers who pulled you over saw the damage to your grille, and Detroit Forensics found blood and brains on the car. Those plates, which were reported stolen, belonged to a car seen in front of a house where a murder took place New Year's Eve or early New Year's Day. That's two killings we can tie you to. You can plead Man Two for Thompson, but the first victim was shot to death at point-blank range. In this state that's a life sentence — without parole, and believe me, they make you behave yourself in places where the death penalty's out of the equation — but you don't have to worry about that, because I'm looking to shackle you to a federal homicide. That's lethal injection.

"It's just like a visit to the doctor," she said. "They even dab your arm with alcohol, in case you might catch infection in the forty seconds before the cyanide shuts down the muscles you need to breathe. You choke to death, just as if they put a rope around your throat and let you strangle; they don't even break your neck like in the old days. *Snap!*" She snapped her fingers, sharp as a sonic boom; Ataman flinched. "There's the thing, clean and quick, only it's too hard on the spectators, so we did away with it. Not PG-thirteen."

"Lady — Marshal — I haven't been in Iroquois Heights in two years."

"Who said Iroquois Heights?"

She was good. As poker faces go she could fade a department psychiatrist, but when she wanted to she could put a light in her eyes that might as well have been shaped like skulls. I'd seen her turn that on me. It still wakes me up nights. Her fingers were clamping the edge of the table hard enough to dent the veneer.

Ataman's face was as blank as a dead TV screen.

"I follow the news. I know someone reported a car at that guy Gates's place the day before he was killed. If you can do better than that, I'll call a lawyer. If not, put me away on the hit-and-run. If you can."

She took a turn around the room, arms crossed. Her heels drew the tendons in her calves as tight as bowstrings. At length she leaned down and planted her palms flat on the table. Her nostrils spread, like a lioness on the scent.

"Boris —"

"If you call me anything, call me Mr. Ataman."

"Boris, there's a team of experts trained at Quantico at great expense to the taxpayers who are busy digging into your background; digging, digging, sweeping aside the dust, and digging again, like archaeologists in Egypt. When they hook you up with the Ukrainian mob, RICO kicks in. You know what that stands for? 'Roy, I'm Cutting you Open.' "

For the first time he looked confused. "I don't know what that means."

"Not officially. It's the Racketeer Influenced and Corrupt Organizations Act, for the ACLU, though they don't like it any better. Unofficially, it means we can make an end run around the Bill of Rights, hold you indefinitely without bringing charges, and put you on a fast track to the little room with a gurney in it: no lawyer, no Miranda, no habeas corpus; just Boris Ataman, time of death calculated to the second. You're special. Ninety-nine percent of the human population has no idea the exact moment when they'll check out. You'll get the chance to balance your checkbook, make out your will, and memorize your last words. My favorite is Oscar Wilde's: 'Either this wallpaper goes or I do.' I bet you can do better."

His finger stopped tracing the carved initials. He folded his hands.

Thaler pulled another of her thousand faces. She sat back, took a deep breath, let it out; smiled. Washington has a good dental plan. She could be a movie star if she didn't like pinning bugs to a board as much as she did. Now she looked like an older sister.

"Give us some names we can do something with, and we'll let you plead to involuntary manslaughter. You'll be out in five years; less than three, if you get along with the corrections officers. Correct me if I'm wrong, but that sounds way better than the needle.

"I'll answer your next question," she went on. "Witness Protection. I'm sure you've seen *Law and Order* — who can avoid it? It's like *The Golden Girls* on cable, twenty-four-seven, thirty days a month, three hundred and sixty-five days a year — so I don't have to spell it out. We'll give you an attractive white-bread name, your choice, if it's not taken, set you up in some place with a nice climate, get you a job that pays at least as much as you make now, with all the benefits.

"Oh, and we'll keep the Siberian tigers at bay. Honestly, Mr. Ataman, you'll be safer than ninety-nine-point-six percent of the population; more, considering that these days even kindergartners can't count on not being mowed down by a yellow prick with an AK-forty-seven. Hell, I'd snap at it myself if I didn't just sign a two-year lease on a condo on the river. You may even wind up happy you didn't step on the brake when that poor schmuck wandered into the street drunk on his ass.

"What do you say?"

Her eyes, normally brown, glowed golden. I made a note to ask her how she pulled that off.

"I want a lawyer."

Henty blew air; for all of us. "She's good."

"She's the best." Alderdyce yawned. "If I'd known just *how* good, I'd have thrown myself in front of the car that took her from Thirteen Hundred to Virginia. Those bastards don't know what they've got."

"Let's not get ahead of ourselves," I said. "He didn't admit anything."

Alderdyce looked at the wrist where he usually wore a watch, scowled. "I'm going home. Wake me when there's peace in the Middle East."

Nineteen

It was late. Even the stars were asleep under a cloud cover as impenetrable as New Math, and as for streetlights the city can't afford to change the bulbs in the ones that haven't been vandalized for scrap; where they work, that's the place to live, if you can't swing the suburbs. A helicopter shot of the city would look like those satellite pictures of North and South Korea, half sparkling, half black as deep space.

I was sleepier than I was hungry, but I stopped at a party store, selected a hot dog that didn't look as if it had been revolving since Christmas, and bought a half-pint of chocolate milk to wash it down in the car. The clerk, a lonely looking Arab with terminal five o'clock shadow, wished me a happy new year, but it seemed to me we were past the cutoff date for that, so I just grunted. I felt bad after. I was paying it backward.

A DPD black-and-gold fell in behind me on McDougall, hung there for a couple of blocks, close enough to read my plate and long enough for the onboard computer to give me a pass, then made a Y-turn and went back the way it had come. It was one of those nights; no late-breaking crime news on the radio, no candlelight vigils, no recent Middle East atrocities to protest, nothing to break the monotony of the midnight tour. It happens sometimes, even in Detroit. I finished my dinner and stuffed all the litter into the sack.

Back at the house I tried Barry Stackpole's cell. He's my go-to for anything that requires a mouse and a keyboard, and up-to-date dope on organized crime. He couldn't care less about serial killers or religious fanatics in dynamite cummerbunds, but if more than two guys conspired to loot a woman's lingerie drawer, he was on it.

"Three to conspire," he once said, "that's all it takes, same as owning cats. It all started with a trio of mooks named Luigi, Nunzio, and Giuseppe."

I'd said, "I think you just offended my Italian great-great-grandmother."

"Bullshit. Everyone knows you were spawned. Anyway, it's no longer current, with a Russian mob and a Korean mob and a black Mafia and the boys in Dixie and the Puerto Rican Junior League. There's one in Aberdeen, but no one takes them seriously in those kilts. If Luigi, Nunzio, and Giuseppe had included a copyright attorney along with their criminal lawyers, they could overturn RICO."

It seemed to me I'd heard that somewhere else, possibly from me.

I figured Barry would know more about the Ukrainians than anyone in Minsk; but the call went straight to his mailbox, which was full as usual. He was probably staking out some gambling hell, disguised as a housefly.

I hit End without leaving a message. He never returned them anyway. He only took calls on the portable when a name he trusted popped up. Too many people were looking for him with baseball bats, and too many of those knew how to track a signal. I was one of the few he gave the number to when he ditched his burner for a new one every three months. He still lived out of a suitcase on occasion, on account of the organic parts he'd left behind at an old ATF crime scene. When you look up "investigative reporter" in *Webster's,* you won't find his picture. He's too cagy to advertise.

Surfing the channels, I caught three minutes of some team sport I'd never seen before from some country I couldn't place, and narrated in some language that sounded like an Alvin and the Chipmunks album played backwards, punctuated by a hoarse guttural whenever someone scored; which seemed to happen every couple of seconds. Somewhere in the Third World there was a sports bar where people were cheering and bets were being made. Everything else was reality and reruns, which sounded too much like my day. I turned off the set. The sudden quiet hurt my ears, like the vacuum after a thunderclap.

I found some leftover Gordon's and made a martini, but poured the bottom half into the sink. It was a shameful waste of perfectly good ice cubes. The dark night of the soul is no hour for cocktails with William and Kate. I tried the stereo, but Sarah Vaughan wasn't doing it for me either. She sounded like someone burping the alphabet.

Even that little bit of liquor sat on the party-store hot dog like a rhinoceros with a sprained ankle. I drank part of a Coke and dumped the rest after the gin and vermouth. I couldn't seem to finish anything, including the case I was working on.

I switched on an under-the-counter light

to discourage burglars and went back into the living room to turn off the lamp next to the easy chair. In the abrupt darkness I saw a light where no light belonged.

I thought it was an interior lamp at first, in the house directly across the street on the Hamtramck side, but the place had been empty for weeks, looking for a buyer. They were tearing down half the buildings in the city and the other half they couldn't give away. A reflection, then, but not in the window; some of the local hope for the future of the world had chucked a piece of asphalt through the glass.

I figured out what it was just before it disappeared; the light from my own kitchen, reflected in the lens of a telescope, or more likely a pair of binoculars, just deep enough in the darkness of a vacant building to put the owner's face in shadow. Whoever it was had been looking directly into my house.

Twenty

That woke me up even more than the first cheery hello from the Coke. I went into the bedroom and undressed in the light from the nightstand, just another night owl getting ready for bed. That window faced the same direction as the one in the living room, but I couldn't make out anything through the gauzy curtain. I put out the lamp, lit a cigarette, and lowered it gently into an ashtray after one drag, where the glowing tip would show through the window at about the level of a man smoking in bed. From the bureau I drew some clothes I could barely see in the darkness and put them on, finishing with a pair of black sneakers. Later, when I saw the getup in a mirror, I looked less like James Bond and more like I'd dressed in the dark; but the stripes and checks blended in better than straight black.

If Peeping Tom was any kind of pro, he'd

wait until the cigarette went out before leaving to report, if he had someone to report to. With no one drawing on it I had maybe ten minutes before it burned down to the filter. I took the Smith & Wesson I hadn't carried that day from the drawer in the nightstand and stuck it under my belt on my way back to the kitchen.

That window faced the house next door on my side of the street, but the counter light would make a glow visible from the one opposite mine. I was careful not to pass in front of the light and make a flutter. I let myself out through the side door to the garage, scooping my keys off the hook next to it, just in case.

There my options narrowed. A corner streetlamp illuminated the window, and although the bay door faced away from the deserted house, a partner watching that side would see me go out that direction if I did it the usual way.

So I didn't do it the usual way. I tugged the door up a foot and a half, blocked it with the battery charger I got a lot of use out of in cold weather, and limboed my way out through the gap. Something slipped in my lower back when I levered myself up onto my feet. I was getting too old for subterfuge.

It all took too long. By the time I made it through the strip of darkness between the kitchen window and the house next door, a motor started and a car pulled away from the curb in front of it, traveling without lights. That would be my surveillant, if such a word exists.

Just for the hell of it, I sprinted back to the garage, this time without worry about being seen, wrenched the door up the rest of the way, threw myself into the Cutlass, started it, and shot out, forgetting the battery charger and chipping a tooth when my right front tire knocked it over, bumped up over it, and landed hard on the concrete pad. I spun the wheel to keep from repeating the mistake with the rear tire and guided the car through the narrow gap on the kitchen side to the street my watcher had taken. My next-door neighbor was going to give me hell for that; we shared that strip of grass.

For once I caught a break. I had my lights off, and the only other car in sight had stopped at a signal, the driver being an honest citizen who didn't want to risk being pulled over on a stakeout job. So far he thought he was in the clear. Ukrainians are usually smarter than that; the czars used to pay them tribute. But I was only guessing he was Ukrainian. I collect enemies like Hummel figurines.

We headed downtown. When a DPW truck trundled out of a side street into the block I'd left between us, I switched on my lights.

There were more cars wandering around near the business section, restaurant staff and city workers heading in for the red-eye shift. I blended in with them and followed a pair of tilted taillights right onto First Street. The streetlamps there were working. The lights belonged to a late-model silver-gray Corolla. The license plate bulb wasn't lit; but if the number started with V-A-L, it would be an insult to my intelligence.

The lights of Greektown — especially the neon of the casino — never go out. On nights like that they bathe the bellies of the clouds in candy colors visible for a mile in every direction, like an exploded clown. I could make out architectural details and the occasional rat scurrying after pheasants from the vacant lots in the neighborhoods. A salvage crook ducked out of sight into a doorway, carrying a coil of copper wire. I kept an eye out for urban coyotes, the four-legged kind.

The nerve center of what used to be one of the largest cities in the United States looked as dead as a kidney in a slop bucket. The wind lifted a newspaper section and nudged it down the sidewalk, a devil ray stranded on dry land.

The unexpected movement distracted me. I lost the Toyota in that second; but it had only deserted the street for the curb. The tailpipe smoked creamily in the frigid air, then stopped as the lights went out.

I drove past, timing it so the driver was distracted by his seat belt buckle — I hoped — and parked in a loading zone near the end of the block. I adjusted my side mirror and watched a medium-built figure in a dark-colored parka get out of the car and cross the street, carrying a slim folder. Without looking around, he scampered up a flight of steps, fished out a set of keys, and let himself into the McNamara Federal Building.

That was satisfaction of a kind. I knew he wasn't smart enough for a Cossack.

Twenty-One

I stayed put and smoked part of a cigarette, in case he'd left something in the car and came back out to get it. When I was reasonably sure he'd be inside a while, I got out, popped my trunk, made a selection from the socket set in the toolbox, took out an impact wrench, a ball-peen hammer, wire snips, and eight feet of flat cable; why I had the cable I couldn't remember, except I can't pass anything lying in the road that might be useful. Walked boldly down the street in the direction of the Toyota carrying my tools and cable; just another midnight-shift city worker earning his pension, for anyone left in the city who cared to look out for his neighbors. I thought of the copper thief, and about my defense if I got picked up. But no one showed on foot or on wheels during the short walk, or when I shone my pocket flash on the dark plate screwed above the bumper: It told me nothing. Government surveillance cars don't advertise, although shame on them for not buying American.

The door on the passenger's side was locked, and likely the one on the driver's too. I placed the socket attached to the wrench on the lock, hesitated — destroying federal property is a felony, but they feed you better than in County — then gave it a smart smack with the hammer. I twisted the socket and pulled, drawing out the cylinder. I had the wire snips ready, but no alarm went off when I opened the door. He must have been in a hurry to file his report and go home to bed.

After rigging the cable, I laid the tools carefully in the gutter out of sight and slid into the passenger's seat. The dome light hadn't come on when he'd opened the door, so he'd switched it off like a good little spook, but just to make sure there wasn't an override I reached across and opened the driver's door a couple of inches. The light stayed off. I pulled the door shut.

I found the vehicle registration in the glove compartment, but all my flash told me was the car belonged to Uncle Sam, and I'd known that already. I put it back and shut the lid.

I had a brainstorm. I reached again, this

time to the sun visor above the steering wheel, felt something, and unclipped a driver's license. Some people still do that, and he'd have his government ID on him for most purposes. In the light of the flash a moon face smiled at me under thinning fair hair. I found out George Andrew Gesner was thirty-three, stood five-foot-ten, weighed 215 pounds, and lived in Farmington Hills. I put him back where I found him. Made myself comfortable.

A blue-and-white crept the opposite direction, poking a sidebeam randomly among the scenery, and a few seconds later a barge of a 1969 Mercury cruised the other way, the bass that had replaced the backseat thumping and making the Toyota's windows buzz. The prowl car's beam swiveled that direction after they passed and the speaker went silent. The vehicles went their separate ways. Apart from those distractions I might have been camped out at Point Barrow.

It was still warm in the car. When I felt myself nodding off I opened my door a crack to let in the flinty cold. Just then the glass door at the top of the fed house steps swung open and my guy skipped down, tugging up the hood of his parka. His hands were empty now. I got a glimpse of pale hair and a round face.

He opened the driver's door and flopped down without checking the inside of the car. He must have called in sick the day they taught that.

"Spies these days," I said. "You lost your edge when the Berlin Wall fell."

He jumped half a league, saw my shape in shadow, and made a move toward his coat, which was fastened with snaps to his neck. I could have waited — with that setup I had all night; it made me want to write my congressman — but I wanted to get to bed too. I left my revolver under my belt and gave him a glimpse of the tin star the county used to pass out like toothbrush samples, my thumb over the embossed legend. His hand stopped.

"Agent Gesner, I'm Archibald West. The badge is temporary; gives me better jurisdiction than a city shield, and it limits curiosity. We don't carry any as a rule. Places I've been, a stop-and-frisk can turn into fifteen years in the Taliban Hilton, or my head in a diplomatic pouch."

"How do you know my name?"

"Please." I looked all-knowing; in the darkness a waste of a good facial expression. But someone would have given him my description at least.

"Who are you with?" He had a high, shallow voice. I spotted him an octave for his nervous condition.

"Since they added 'explosives' to Alcohol, Tobacco, and Firearms, I never use it. ATFE sounds like a safety razor."

"What's Treasury got to do with — anyone else?"

He'd caught himself; he hadn't missed class the day they gave Indoctrination. It takes more than an executive order about interagency cooperation to overcome a century of conditioning.

"Never mind that." I snapped on my flash. "Is that an option with this model, or part of the standard equipment?"

He followed the pencil beam to the flat wire running from the underside of the steering column through the crack of the door on the hinge side.

"I don't —"

"Of course not. Who'd drive around with Primacord fixed to his ride? The newer stuff that makes it look like Reddi-wip, but they don't need it to blow a pothole the size of Crater Lake under this car. There wouldn't be enough even for the scrap hounds."

"It looks like ordinary TV antenna wire."

"I'll pass that along. Next time they'll make it round and black with a burning fuse, straight from Acme, so there's no confusion."

"But, why — ?"

"You tell me." I gave it a beat, but he wasn't having any; sighed, as if I were disappointed. "From the position, I'd say it's wired from the steering mechanism to the drive shaft, to go off when you put the car in gear and turn the wheel; but it could be a decoy. Ignition makes a better spark, and there's always the speedometer, set to blow at the mph of choice. Did you see *Speed*?"

"I was only inside a few minutes."

"Irrelevant. Last year, a congressional aide stopped ten seconds to pay the toll in Oklahoma and wound up all over the panhandle. Someone mistook him for his boss. We traced the charge to a member of a NASCAR pit crew. He's in Gitmo now, blowing up water wings."

"We haven't sent anyone there in years."

Jackpot. Whatever division he worked for, it had teeth. "You'd know, probably. They lie to me all the time; but I guess I'm not in your pay grade."

He reached for his door handle. I leaned across him and caught his wrist.

"I wouldn't. He might've rigged a claymore inside the seat, to explode when you lift your weight off it."

"Jesus!"

He let go of the handle and I released my grip. He was hyperventilating now. He snatched open his coat. My hand went automatically toward my belt. He came out with a plastic inhaler, shook it, stuck it in his mouth, and pumped. When he took it out he was breathing normally — for a man who thought he was sitting on a bomb. He had even me feeling nervous.

"Why me?" he said again.

"What are you working on?"

"That's classified."

I chuckled and slapped him on the shoulder. He tried to give the car a sunroof with his head.

"Good man, Gesner. You'll get the flags at half-mast. Do me a favor and stay put for five minutes. I'm putting my kid through Columbia." I opened my door.

This time it was my arm in the vise. "Aren't you going to disarm it?"

"I'll have to call a team. I'm only trained to spot them, not put them out of action. The union might get sore."

"Well, call them!"

"They're not the fire department. They don't just come on my word. I could be an imposter, or gone over. Without something they can check, they'll stay put rather than charge into an ambush. Who's your assignment?"

"How do you know it's a who?"

"I don't fly solo, George. The whole reason behind Homeland is all the agencies share information, up to a point. We know you're surveilling someone in the area" — *surveilling,* I was pretty sure he'd approve of that — "and that you just came in from your shift to report. Who's the pigeon?"

He drummed his fingers on the inhaler in his lap. "Local private detective named Walker, Amos Walker."

"Why?"

"I don't know why, that's need-to-know. I'm just supposed to stake out his place, follow him if necessary, and report on his movements. That's it."

I reached up and ran a hand along the headliner.

"What are you doing?"

"Sometimes they plant napalm canisters under the roof. They're only about the size of a thirty-five-millimeter film container, but they take out the guess factor. The day after nine-eleven, a GSA accountant survived a whole case of C-4, so they upped the ante."

"Jesus!" He crossed himself.

"Relax. There's nothing up there. Somebody doesn't think you're important enough to stretch the budget."

"I'm not important at all."

I fished out my cell. "I'll make the call. Sit tight for the crew."

"How long will *that* take?"

"Twenty minutes is the record. That was Hamilton, a legend in the District; but he's in Yemen now, and anyway that was before the underwear bomber. You might be in luck, though. We've got more men assigned to Dearborn than Washington, and that's just next door. All those Arabs, you know? You didn't hear that from me. We don't profile no more. Who do you report to?"

"Nobody."

"Who was the folder for? We've been watching you a while, George."

"That was the day's log. I seal it in a pouch and put it in a pigeonhole with a number on it."

I didn't ask for the number. I wasn't about to compound the felony by breaking into the federal building.

"One last question. How do you know this character Walker when you see him?"

"We snagged his photo from the state police file on private investigators. He doesn't look like anyone special, but I know him when I see him. He keeps weird hours,

I can tell you that."

"As opposed to you," I snapped. I didn't appreciate that nothing-special crack.

"Especially lately." He took another hit from the inhaler; that set his brain working. "What if there's a timer? I'm supposed to sit here waiting to find out?"

"Which you never will, either way."

"Oh, Jesus. Oh, Christ." He'd gone so white I could see his face clearly in the dark.

I took pity on him then. He was a tadpole in a tank full of barracuda. I knew how that felt.

"George?"

"What?"

I pointed my flash under my chin and snapped it on.

His mouth opened, but not for the inhaler. "Hey! You're —"

I grinned.

"Go home, George. I'm leaving you the wire as a present. It was a rescue job; I'm a pack rat. But I don't know what to do with it since my cable company replaced flatwire with fiber-optic." I opened the door and let myself out.

He was still sitting there putting it all together when I made a U-turn and passed him going the other way. In a little while he was going to get mad. Maybe even mad enough to report the incident.

Chances were no. When he found the ruined lock, he'd replace it on his own dime rather than admit he'd been taken in by a common P.I.; but I'd been disappointed before. At least I knew whoever he was reporting to wasn't with Treasury, or he wouldn't have asked what its interest was. That ought to bring comfort eating London broil in the correctional facility up in Milan.

Twenty-Two

I undressed completely and slid between the sheets, but sleep's like chasing unicorns when your back's aching, your bad leg's hurting worse than always, your heart's thumping like the bass in the back of a '69 Merc, and your brain's racing down a ninety-degree slope with the brakes out.

In other words, a typical night in the romantic life of the private eye; I'd been tanked, threatened, schmoozed, followed, and cornered into committing a federal crime — one, at least. What George Andrew Gesner chose to make of it in a civil case concerning pain and suffering was up to him and a slew of courts.

Nothing made sense. An ordinary citizen — assuming that creature still existed outside the Museum of Natural History — had been shot to death in his basement, the Ukrainian mob was involved (or maybe not), the Episcopal Church was offering blood money for the person or persons responsible, two more murders had logged in, the feds were involved, I was in their gun sights, a hyperactive kid was giving screwy answers to even screwier questions, a solid citizen (see above) was feeding out disinformation about the first victim's associations — and there was even a stoic Indian. It was like a collaboration between Robert Ludlum, Zane Grey, Rod Serling, and the writers of an after-school special.

It all seemed like a lot for a job that had started out with me listening to fuzzy tapes and making cold calls.

But that was the nature of the work: A prospective client drops in, you ask him to sit down, offer him refreshment, sit back in your swivel with your eyes closed and your hands tented under your chin like Sherlock Holmes, and listen to his life's history, making no judgments, because you've heard it all before, like an old priest trying to pay attention and not think about that charter-boat service for sale in Florida, or the mom-and-pop bookstore in Indiana struggling against Amazon, or the corner saloon in Toledo, or in my case the small Minnesota town looking for a police chief; some quiet, out-of-the-way place that exists only in reruns of *The Andy Griffith Show.* More unicorns. So you crank yourself out of bed when the alarm rings, sip two cups of strong coffee in your breakfast nook over the morning paper — another doomed institution — shave, shower, drive to the office, go through the circulars, past-due notices, and letters threatening dire consequences for breaking the chain, set fire to an unlawful cigarette, and wait for the buzzer that would let in the next prospect. Who knows? He might be a dictator in exile, looking for a place to spend the nation's treasury he managed to pack in his suitcase before the doors crashed in, or a movie star offering gross points in his next blockbuster in return for following you around for a day and learning all the secrets of your trade.

Or a suddenly single mother wanting to know who killed her husband and why it was so important it was worth destroying her world.

You spend most of your time studying dusty records under a sixteen-watt bulb and the wary eye of a minimum-wage civil servant, dialing phones and crossing out numbers, sitting in a car with the engine off in all extremes of weather, playing with a cigarette you can't light and staring at the door of some building until your eyes water and you swear it's opening, but it isn't, and when it does you almost miss it, because your brain went out for a walk and left your body behind. Why it came back at all was just habit.

You never know where the spoor will lead; to a big payoff, a dead stop, a crack on the skull, a cop with brass knuckles for brains, a gangbanger with his veins full of horse and only you standing between him and his next hit — it was always the amateurs that got you, ask any dead gunslinger — a slug in the back and a pimple-faced M.E. eating an egg-salad sandwich over your entrails on a table. Every P.I. has faced enough melodrama to fill a book, if not quite a series like the heroes of fiction. The amount you meet is scary enough. But if routine follow-up was all the work offered, I'd just as soon teach ballroom dancing to quadriplegics.

If only it weren't for all that government green gnawing its way to the surface. It didn't matter how many coats of beige and sky blue and rose you slapped on top of it; it started as a haze, like crabgrass, and before you knew what was happening you were in it up to your knees.

The telephone rang, a welcome shock treatment.

"Sorry about the hour."

Lewellyn Hale's voice, crisp as a crumpet. "Four o'clock there, isn't it?"

"Not that bad." I stood naked in the living room, shivering in sixty degrees. I'd turned down the thermostat before piling in a half hour before. "Michigan's in the Eastern Time Zone. I can't seem to get that into people's heads."

"Really. I must make a note of that. I'm an insomniac. I thought you might be one also."

"Only when acted upon by outside forces. Don't they have sleeping pills up there?"

"And lose my edge? I consider my affliction an advantage over the average bloke."

"So bloody English, so bloody early. Where are you from, really?"

"They tell me I was born in Southampton, while my parents were waiting for the boat to the States. I lived with them till I was thirty. Hard to scrape off the fish-and-chips after all that mollycoddling. Okay, pal," he said, in a questionable imitation of Steve McQueen. "I wanted to report while it was all fresh. It's never the same when I'm reading from notes, for some reason. The wink-winks in between wipe out all the intuitive impressions."

"Hang on."

I put down the handset, fetched a robe,

and switched on the coffeemaker. The gurgling helped. I lit up my first of the day; or maybe it was the last of the day before. Back in the living room I picked up.

"Fire away. In American, please. It took me five years to get though *David Copperfield.*"

"What that man did to the King's English should have put him in the dock. I talked to Chuck Swingline. The Ojibway?"

"I was just thinking about him, in an abstract way."

"An ordeal. My man in Ottawa got on his bad side right at the start, addressing him as a Native American. Swingline spent five minutes explaining why no Indian worthy of his heritage would appreciate being called American. You chaps really did a number on the aborigines."

"So did you Canucks. The Mexicans too. And let's not forget the British. I read somewhere they were the ones who taught them how to take scalps."

"Balls. One of the first sights the pilgrims recorded was a row of Huron topknots waving in the breeze from Iroquois lances. I didn't call you to discuss the history of genocide."

"You started it. Hang on once more."

The machine had finished gurgling. I

snatched out the carafe, scalding the back of my hand on the stream still coming out, filled a cup, and sipped from it on my way back.

"Fire away."

"Malroux — that's my man, he's from Montreal — caught up with Swingline ice fishing clear up on Lake Nipigon, which is where polar bears go to cool off; the plane fare will be on the bill. Crazy former bush pilot named Eagan, with a steel pin in every bone in his body. Swingline had fourteen tip-ups going. That's more than Caucasians are allowed by law, but the tribal lawyers make sure the treaties are honored."

I sat down in the easy chair. "What was the temp?"

"Twenty below, by your measure. There may be a surcharge for treatment of frost-bite."

"What was Swingline wearing?"

"Wearing? I — oh." I could hear him blush. "I am guilty of over-reporting. Assign it to forty-one hours without a wink."

"We're all tired. Continue."

"Swingline's not the garrulous type, and I don't suppose time in that rough country polished his social skills. He told Malroux he only visited that hunting lodge with Gates and the rest because they were footing the bill; to be able to tell the folks back home they hunted with a real Indian, I imagine. He considered Rudy Johnson the only real hunter in the pack, and he was a drunk — not, I suspect, that that part bothered him. Swingline had a six-pack of Moosehead keeping cold in all fourteen holes and he drank two at every stop while Malroux was following him around. You'd think they'd make some effort to avoid the stereotype."

"What about Gates?"

"Had to be reminded who he was. The fellow doesn't seem to have made much of an impression, but then I don't suppose the old boy's faculties can be trusted at the bottom of that ocean of beer. There wasn't much point to asking him if he had any idea who killed Gates, but of course the question was asked. Do I need tell you the answer?"

"Where was he New Year's Eve?"

"Trapping beaver up on Hudson's Bay, just like you read in books. My opinion? He had a stash of liquor, and possibly a warm companion to share it with. Ojibways make a killing selling genuine pelts to Yanks on holiday; some of them even came from this side of China. We confirmed his story with the proprietor of a picturesque trading post in Fort George — bearskins, spears, convincing arrowheads, all that rot — who sold him four cases of Moosehead New Year's Day."

"He could have caught a plane."

Hale chuckled. No U.S. citizen could do it the same justice.

"It just so happens I thought of that. An Alberta Clipper tore through that morning, dumping a meter of snow by noon and closing every airport from Toronto on up to Baffin Island. Even that maniac Eagan wouldn't go out in it; he was shacked up with his half-Inuit wife in a cabin in Winnipeg. You Yanks haven't quite managed to cock up the climate up here just yet."

"I'm bleeding; really, I am. You just can't hear it from this distance. I hope you got all this over the phone."

The air stiffened on his end.

"I'm a religious man, Walker. I don't fritter away church money."

"Don't be so cranky just because you didn't get enough sleep." I fingered a cigarette. "I wonder why Perlberg said Swingline and Gates were close?"

"Is that an assignment?"

"No, just guessing out loud. Thanks, Lulu. Look me up next time you're in town."

"If you promise not to call me Lulu."

I didn't go back to bed after we finished talking. I never lighted the cigarette. Gray was bleeding into the black outside, and I was wide awake. I had time before the city woke up to make a decent breakfast to dump on top of last night's leaden hot dog and chase it with a gallon of black coffee. I could actually smell the pancakes when I fell asleep in the chair, and when I woke up the sun was strong for winter.

I needed to start making visits.

Dressing after my shower and shave, I glanced through the bedroom window at the empty house across the street, and that's when I realized it had snowed. It had started sometime after I'd dozed off, fluffy as baby chicks, and by the time the sun broke through it was piled nearly to the sill of the window George Gesner had stood behind. The first real sun in days struck sparks off it like stripper dust.

It was painful to look at in the strong light. When I turned my head away, green-and-purple balloons floated inside my pupils as if someone had popped an old-fashioned flashbulb in my face at point-blank range.

I hadn't seen anyone inside the house. I wondered if George was back on duty or if there was a day man, and if he'd be the one who'd follow me when I left. I'm not so stuck on myself I expect Washington to spend that much of its budget on me; but an institution that would pay two hundred bucks for a twelve-dollar pipe wrench is capable of anything.

TWENTY-THREE

The announcer was reciting a long list of school closings when I flipped on the car radio. I listened impatiently; it was like being a kid again and your school always seemed to be the last to call in. When Iroquois Heights came up, I pointed the hood that way and called Amelie Gates.

"Good morning, Mr. Walker. No, I'm afraid Michel isn't home. He's spending the day with a friend."

"Can you tell me where? I want to ask him a couple of things."

"No, I can't let you do that without me present. You understand." She went on without pause, almost tripping over her words. "I really can't talk now. I'm late for Belle Isle."

"Sure you can make it?"

"I have to. As bad as it is for me, it's worse for those poor people on the island."

"I'll pick you up. I've been driving in this

stuff since I was sixteen."

"No, there's no —"

I hung up as if I hadn't heard her. I didn't like the way she sounded. It all made sense, but she hadn't had to speak at 78 rpm to make her point. A truth told at lying speed might as well be a lie.

She must have been watching through a window. I'd barely got stopped, sliding a little in the wet snow, when she came out wearing her old quilted coat and man's checked hunting cap with a tote bag over her shoulder and let herself into the passenger's seat. I asked her what kept her going.

"This," she said, drumming her fingers on the bag in her lap, as if that meant something more than just jangled nerves. "All this. It's more than just avoiding sitting around, dwelling on things. When I see those people literally fighting to survive — I don't mean just men and women, but small children, who did nothing to deserve what's happened to them — I'm reminded I'm not the only one in the world with sorrows."

She looked down, smiled, and turned her head my way. "I don't suppose there was anything original in that. I heard it myself, before — well, before. But it's like falling in love for the first time and suddenly understanding what all the songs are about." She returned her attention to the windshield. "Have you ever been in love, Mr. Walker?"

"I was married."

"Not an answer."

"Then the answer is I don't know."

"I'll accept that. People who say you know when it's real don't know what they're talking about. I honestly don't know if I loved Don. He was a good man, and I was comfortable with him, but not so much recently. He seemed to be drifting away. It's not the same as when you asked if he was acting differently; he just — he wasn't always *there.* They say that's not unusual after a certain number of years, but —"

"Yeah. They don't know what they're talking about. Drifted away how?"

"Not important. Mr. Walker, I want you to quit this investigation."

"Uh-huh." I slowed almost to a stop behind a city snowplow, scraping the white stuff into rusty clumps on the sidewalk, then powered around it when the opposite lane opened.

"You're not surprised?"

"A little, but only because that usually comes later. At one time or another, just about every client loses interest. You got used to the way something was, so you try to do something about it. Then you get so you're used to the way it is. This seems early. But everyone has his own timeline."

"I just want for Michel and me to be left alone. It was horrible enough, then when the church offered that reward it became grotesque. The reporters block their numbers when they call, so when one doesn't come up I let it ring. When the machine kicks in and they don't leave a message, I know I was right."

"Either that or someone wanted to sell you something."

"Anyway," she said, folding her hands on the bag, "the police will go on looking. I happen to have more faith in them than some people with money."

"It's not as simple as that. You're not the client."

"Reverend Melville is an understanding woman. If she knows how much it means to us, I'm sure she'll agree, and withdraw the offer."

"Again, not that simple. The only one who can take it down is the donor who put it up, and she won't budge on who it is."

"Can you talk to her, at least? I can't imagine her resisting the wishes of a widow and her child."

I drove for a little.

"This got anything to do with my wanting to talk to Michel?"

"It does, in a way. I don't want him drawn into this. He's lost his father, there's nothing that can be done about that now. But I can prevent him from losing his privacy."

"Little boys can't spell privacy, much less know what it means. They write their names in the snow in public."

"Well, sense of security. Even after it's all over, solved or not, the press keeps calendars. Every big anniversary they scrounge up an old story and play it up with bright colors. It could haunt him all his life, as if he peaked at age ten and all the rest was follow-up. They can turn a person into a freak."

"I'll talk to Melville. No promises."

"Thank you. That's all I ask."

We rumbled over the MacArthur Bridge, hung with icicles like something out of Nordic legend, and I let her out near the volunteer tent. The homeless stood or crouched in the snow, dark lumps with red faces, some smoking, others messing with smart phones; you wondered where the bills were sent.

Maybe they just needed the distraction. In any case it was none of my business. My business was why Amelie Gates wanted to pull the plug.

The wind was blowing my way. I smelled corn chowder and Tater Tots, and remembered I hadn't had time for breakfast after all. I stopped for an Egg McMuffin and a towering cup of blistering hot coffee on my way to Christ Episcopal Church. Waiting at the drive-through and again when I pulled out I watched the rearview mirror, but it looked like George Gesner's day-shift replacement hadn't clocked in. That's how it looked.

"You know, if it weren't for people needing to get in and out, I'd leave the stuff where it is. Sometimes I wonder if I'm just interfering with God's plan."

Florence Melville leaned on a square-bladed shovel on the front steps of the church on Jefferson; snow piled the flower bed hibernating on either side. She wore what looked like a man's army greatcoat, but the sleeves fit and the hem came just to the tops of her galoshes. Sturdy as she'd looked sitting at her desk, upright she topped six feet.

"Can it wait?"

She stopped leaning. "Has something happened? A break in the case?"

"You've been watching *Law and Order* when you should be watching the Religious Channel. Can we go inside? My heater's on the fritz. I've forgotten what my feet felt like."

Her office looked the same as before; even the light quality hadn't changed. It was an island in the sea of time.

"You do look a little gray," she said, opening a carved square in the paneling. "Is it too early for brandy?"

"Not if you join me."

"Just a sip." She filled two cut-glass snifters from a matching decanter filled with liquid the color of old gold and brought them to the desk. Mine was empty before she sat down. Her brows lifted. "You're not supposed to drink it like that. It was a gift from a parishioner. It's thirty years old."

"It's old enough to go out on its own."

"Would you like another?"

I shook my head. "The Widow Gates wants you to give me my walking papers."

"Just how soon did she expect results?"

"It isn't that. It isn't what she said it was, either, that she wants to get on with her life. It all started when I asked her a second time if I could talk to her son."

"That little boy? What could he know?"

"They're not kittens. They're born with

their eyes open."

"What do you suspect?"

"Too early. It's not like drinking brandy. I promised her I'd ask." I found a comfortable position in the medieval chair and rested my hands on the scrolled arms. "I'm not quitting. I could make the case that I'm still halfway employed by the sheriff's department, but if you can me and it gets back to them they'll have an excuse to cut me loose. Lieutenant Henty tried once already."

"You're not a very popular man, are you?" She took a sip, swallowed, turned her glass around by the stem, took another. "I want you to stay on, of course. At the same time —"

"You don't want to rock any personal boats. In answer to your question: No, I'm not Big Man on Campus with a lot of people. You get used to it."

"Well, I'd rather not do *that;* I have a board to answer to, and as I said, the Gateses were very generous to this church. Is it all right if I think about it?"

"That's the *B* answer, but I'll take it; if you promise to take your time."

She leaned forward without seeming to move. "You're on to something, aren't you? The end is in sight."

"No. Something else has moved in to block it. Which is encouraging, because it means there *is* an end."

"Is there danger involved?"

"Three people are dead who should be walking around. You tell me."

She emptied her glass and got up to pour refills for us both.

TWENTY-FOUR

We spent the rest of the visit talking about the Tigers' chances next season and I left, still part of the workforce.

Sitting at the curb scraping the winey aftertaste off my tongue with my teeth, I ran my options. Before I could talk myself out of the first one I came to I started the motor and headed for Centerline. I wanted to ask Richard Perlberg why he'd sent me off on a wild–Canada goose chase about such buddies Donald Gates and Chuck Swingline were.

His building was still redbrick, still situated on a straight section of track imported from Indianapolis Speedway; but this time the timing of the stoplights came through and I got a space a block down without risking a fender.

The middle-aged receptionist was on the phone. She recognized me when she hung up. "Are you here for Richard? I don't" —

she checked her book.

"No appointment this time. I just need a minute."

"I'm sorry. He took a personal day."

"Can I get him at home?"

"He said something about going ice fishing up north."

I thanked her and turned to leave. She swiveled, reaching for a stack of papers on a credenza. With her back turned I scuttled down the hall toward the office. I slipped the spring latch with a thin steel strip I carry in my wallet, let myself in, and closed the door behind me quickly, easing the latch into the frame.

There was enough light coming through the window to give the place a good frisking. I didn't know what I was looking for, a cooked book or the Hope diamond or what was left of Jimmy Hoffa, but I didn't find anything I wouldn't expect to find in a bean counter's place of business.

Which was suspicious enough. Everyone has something that doesn't fit. If I were a man with a secret and I was fixing to cut out for a long spell I'd get rid of the porno and Air Supply CDs, but there wasn't anything even half that criminal. None of the detective's manuals say anything about looking for the thing that isn't there.

I stood there a while hands on hips, looking around, then went back to the door. I was turning the knob when something caught the corner of my mind's eye. I went back to the desk and picked up Perlberg's electric stapler. The brand name was embossed on the handle: SWINGLINE.

"Sir?"

But I was passing the receptionist's desk too fast, and went out the door.

The tail this time was a blue Chrysler; it stayed with me for six blocks, never falling more than five lengths behind, until I caught a ripe yellow light, left it sitting, and made a right and a left and a right again, stairstepping to make sure I'd lost it. I was fresh out of fake Primacord, and anyway I didn't feel like another masquerade.

It hadn't been there on my way to Centerline, which meant I'd picked it up at Perlberg's building. Maybe it had something to do with that audit he was working on.

I dialed my cell.

"Yeah."

"Walker, Barry. Most people say 'Hello.' "

"Telephone etiquette went out with the Yellow Pages. Whatever it is, can it wait? I just this minute got back from Aspen."

"You *ski*?"

"This isn't your father's prosthetic. I'm thinking of having the other leg lopped off and getting a matched set. I'm wiped. I just want to finish eating my fish and hit the sheets."

"It'll take just a minute."

"Longer than that, if you can't talk over a cell." A long breath let out. "The Blue Heron."

It was in Birmingham, with reservations stacked up like Friday air traffic. Barry Stackpole had a table waiting for him every day until closing; a party named Paulie Rock of Ages had been soaking the owner for protection until Barry had offered to sweep Paulie's house for bugs every month for a year in return for taking his business elsewhere. The owner was grateful.

The restaurant offered free Wi-fi, whatever that was, and Barry's table was in the sweetest spot in the joint. He was polishing off a plate of Atlantic salmon and washing it down with a Corona when I sat down opposite him. He was beginning to show age for the first time since I'd known him. In order to pass for a college freshman, he'd have to make up some story about a two-year tour in Iraq. His fair face was tanned the color of Florence Melville's brandy, which made his blue eyes more startling than usual. He pushed aside his plate with the hand that still had all its fingers, reached across to shake mine, and sat back, drawing a smart phone from the flap pocket of a flannel shirt.

"Who'm I hacking today?" he asked.

"You can do that from that itty thing?"

"I'll never make the younger generation understand it used to take a warehouse to hold a computer and it couldn't keep up with a *Dora the Explorer* model."

"I wouldn't know how to use the Dora. I can't figure out how to put my phone on vibrate."

"If that's why you're keeping me out of a nice soft bed, you can pick up the tip."

"If I want my pants to buzz I'd put a bee in my pocket. I'm government bait this season."

"That why you look like shit?"

"No, but it's sweet of you to notice." I told him about George Andrew Gesner. He thumbed some buttons, waited, frowned. "Nada. Which backs your story. Only a spook can keep his name off the Big Eye. Did you really tell him you're ATF?"

I grinned into the general atmosphere: muted, only half full at that hour, with Bacharach leaking out of invisible speakers and discreet waiters setting tables for the lunch rush. "I think they're too busy rounding up stray pressure cookers to tank me. Gesner's twins; or maybe not. I picked up some more interest this morning, but I don't know if it's government. On the other hand, I haven't been back in circulation long enough to start collecting a variety of shadows."

"The clink?"

"Rehab."

He looked at me. I opened a palm. "I was past due. I'm all right now. Just a little sore from shots."

"See any celebrities?"

"Just fat Elvis. All I know for sure is this isn't Treasury. George as much as told me that flat out."

"Anything in this for me?"

"For a while it looked like the Ukrainian mob, but it's beginning not to."

"We'll come back to that. Get the plate?"

I gave him the number. He entered it. While he was waiting for a hit I asked him if he wasn't worried about eavesdropping.

He spent some time stroking the screen. "Not anymore. Right after I bought this I took it to an old friend who used to be in Mossad. The Israelis are light years ahead of everyone else in intel when it comes to electronics. They make Mitsubishi look like

Fisher-Price."

"They got a Mafia over there?"

"What, I'm not allowed to hang out with somebody not connected to my business?"

"You are, but you don't."

"Fuck you, Jack. Yeah, scratch any kibbutz and you'll find a wiseguy who orders his meatballs without pork sausage. Mazel tov to me," he said, turning the screen my way.

I read what was written there, sat back, took a pull off his beer bottle, and swallowed loudly. "I'll be damned."

"That's between you and your spiritual adviser. You owe me a beer."

Twenty-Five

He signaled the waiter for his beer. "Tell me about the Ukrainians."

"What, you don't want to talk about this?" I waved a hand at his vest-pocket ENIAC.

"Nothing to talk about, without hacking into Washington, and I'm not going to do that wearing a bag over my head. Spill."

I waited until the beer came and the waiter left. Then I gave the particulars. Just laying them out made me dizzy.

"I passed one of those billboards on the way back from the airport," he said. "That's one of the things I planned to poke into when I sat down. Yuri Yako?"

"He was born Yuri Crowley. The marshals changed it."

"Doesn't ring a bell. Must be low-level. Don't know Boris, but I know some Atamans. Fyodor sold out all his local interests when things got hot and went back home. Either he forgot he was wanted there or he thought things had changed since the Iron Curtain rusted through. Some things haven't. They walked him down a hallway in Lubyanka Prison and put a slug from a Vostok in his brain."

"He have a son?"

"One of the things he was wanted for was practicing homosexuality."

"They execute you for that?"

"Not since capitalism. He cut off his lover's head with a saber he inherited from his great-grandfather."

"Where do you get this stuff?"

"Officially speaking, I don't have it. State Department offered Witness Protection, but he decided to take his own chances. His file's sealed."

"You hacked it?"

"FOIA kills trees. I'm an environmentalist."

"How do you stay off the no-fly list?"

He took his turn grinning.

"What, I don't have friends? He might have inherited his sexual persuasion along with the saber. Those old steppe winters were seven months long."

"Still, he could have a kid."

He mashed some keys, massaged the screen, read, turned it around. He'd brought up what looked like a corporate executive chart, with a Vladislav Ataman at the top and more branches than Starbucks. There were two Borises, but from the dates they'd been dead since before the October Revolution.

"I seem to remember something about a Boris raping a sister with the Eastern Orthodox Church under one of the czars," he said; "at a guess, it's not a cherished moniker in the family. Well, occupation names like Ataman are like Smith and Wheeler here. Fyodor's the only one who mobbed up."

"Maybe this Boris is a street soldier, like Yako."

"If any other Ataman had anything to do with Mafiasky, he'd be in my program. I keep up with all the little buds on the family trees. Somebody's pulling your leg about the mob thing."

"The one I know recruited civilians from time to time. Yako's computer showed drug activity. Maybe he and Boris were running an indy operation."

"Shit." He pressed another key. A chorus of "Rags to Riches" played him off-line. It was the *Goodfellas* theme. "Now I've got to start a new file. I feel like J. Edgar Hoover."

We finished both his beers and we stood

and shook hands again. He looked as tired as he said he was. If he'd really gone skiing, odds were he'd shared a hot toddy with the acting head of Murder, Incorporated.

He didn't let go of my hand right away. "You sure you're all right? I went through a patch myself."

"I remember."

"That was just booze. This was further back, after they stitched me back together. I made friends with every pharmacist in the western hemisphere."

"I'm holding my own."

"You know who else said that? The captain of the *Edmund Fitzgerald.* It was his last transmission."

I went to the McNamara Federal Building, this time in broad daylight. Apart from the fact I had some questions to ask, it was probably the only place in the city where I wouldn't pick up a government tail. It's a psychological no-man's-zone, like double-parking in front of Detroit Police Headquarters.

It's a hollowed-out granite block without a single original architectural idea to distract the occupants from their work. Even the name was slapped on as an afterthought, to honor a corrupt county executive on the occasion of his death.

I left the Chief's Special in the car, but a ballpoint pen set off the metal detector anyway. Within ten minutes, everyone in the building would know what was in my pockets.

The directory led me to Mary Ann Thaler's office on the third floor. She'd graduated from the closet where they used to keep the copying machine to a room with a window, with her name lettered on a plastic strip beside the door; she was just one promotion away from a metal sign. No one answered my knock and the door was locked. Everyone was busy ice fishing that day.

I hit the jackpot when the elevator doors opened and she was standing there, this time wearing a wool cap with a button on top and an all-weather coat that glistened like a seal's. She looked fresh as buttered toast.

"If it isn't Jimmy Valentine," she said. "Did you bring your burglar tools?"

Twenty-Six

I hesitated with my thumb still poised above the button. "I didn't peg Gesner for a company man."

"He didn't initiate the report. His section chief hit him up for a lift and spotted the punched-out lock on the passenger's side. Gesner didn't know it was there."

"Whose bright idea was it to put him in the field?"

"The situation has been corrected."

"By you?"

"I don't hire or fire. The day they ask me to do that is the day I give notice."

We were walking down the hall now toward her office. "I should have known he was one of yours, but I didn't think the marshals were that hard up."

"NSA gets first pick. You've seen the news. They know who we're interviewing." Stopping at her door, she produced a glossy card with nothing printed on it and scanned it above the lock. The LED flashed green and she held the door for me.

"Ladies first."

She stood her ground. "Say that again and I'll add obstruction of justice to all the other charges. That one sticks when all the others fall away."

I went in ahead of her. A lamp with a brushed-steel shade came on when she flipped a switch. The walls were paneled in charcoal and chalk arranged in vertical stripes with the texture of burlap. Crossing the gunmetal carpet was like walking on a bed of nails.

She saw me looking at the desk, a giant curling stone. "Are you intimidated?"

"Petrified." I pointed my chin at a photo in a frame on the desk showing the lighthouse at Ludington at sunset. In that setting the orange was bright enough to scorch your eyes. "That didn't come with the office."

"I took it myself, last fall. The place was beginning to intimidate *me.*"

She got rid of her hat, shook loose her hair, and sat down, shrugging out of the coat in a graceful gesture that left it draped over the back of her chair. She wore a plain red wool dress that fit her as snugly as a swimsuit, no jewelry, little makeup. Her chair was upholstered in gray Naugahyde, the one on my side not at all. It was a granite-colored scoop with a steering-wheel base. I felt like p.i. on the half-shell.

"Place bugged?"

"Of course not." She mouthed the word "Yes."

"I don't guess it would matter if it was. You've already got me booked on the Alcatraz Express."

She slid open a file drawer in the desk, withdrew a gray cardboard folder, opened it, and put on a pair of reading glasses with steel frames. They made her look like the sexy librarian I remembered from before ocular surgery. "You graduated from Vicodin to Percodan, and from seventy-five grams to a hundred and fifty. Your blood-sugar level is one hundred and twenty. You're plainly not porked up on Clark bars, so it's probably alcohol abuse."

"Is that my medical record? What happened to HPPA?"

"That's just a suggestion, like the Bill of Rights." She snapped shut the file and took off the specs. In the light coming through the single window her brown eyes had gold flecks. "We've put in for a court order attaching Dr. Jeanne Miernik's notes on your session with her."

"Jeannie," I corrected. "As in 'meany.' Except she's a doll. Actually, I plan to ask her if I can quote her in my advertising. According to her I'm the only person in America who doesn't need to have his head examined. You should've stuck with the guy who tailed me there and put Gesner to work emptying wastebaskets."

"Gesner was the night man. We used the first string because you're more dangerous during the day, when all the offices are open. Or were, until you committed three felonies in front of this building."

"Breaking-and-entering and lying to a federal officer. What's the third?"

"Threatening his life."

"With antenna wire? It wasn't even fiber-optic."

"The case can be made. It's his story against yours."

"He's a natural for cross-examination." I got out a cigarette. She opened her mouth to say something predictable, but I just walked the cigarette across the back of my hand. "What makes me Lady Di to your paparazzi?" I asked.

She stood and put on her coat. "Let's go for a walk."

I thought from the coat we were going outside, but we took the fire stairs and stopped at the next landing. It was cold enough to see our breath.

"The District," she said, hugging herself. "Pay three hundred bucks for a toilet seat and save on heating and electronic surveillance in the stairwells. If you repeat this conversation, I'll hit you with all three charges and as many more as we can dream up. Terrorism, how's that? Leaking official secrets that can make their way back to the enemy."

"Put me on the stand."

"Old-fashioned thinking. We can keep it from going to trial for years while your lawyer files appeal after appeal for bail. Speedy and public? Everything's relative."

I was still holding the cigarette. I put it to its intended use, blowing the smoke away from her. It seemed to warm the air. I shook out the match. "Okay. If it doesn't get in the way of my thing."

A daddy longlegs scampered between us. Thaler's reflexes were faster. She scraped the sole of her shoe on the edge of a step. "That drug activity we found on Yako's computer contained a link to Donald Gates's modem. They were working together."

"Sure Yako wasn't trying to lay it off on him?"

"We eliminated that first thing. We have one of those programs that traces vocabulary and style patterns, like the one the *New York Times Book Review* uses to expose established writers publishing so-called first novels under pseudonyms."

"That's how they found out Mickey Spillane wrote Shakespeare."

"Mickey wasn't bloody enough; but you're catching on. Gates's e-mails with Yako were unsigned, and he was savvy enough to cover his tracks, but our program compared the communications with his regular business correspondence and got a hit. It would hold up in court; but that's a moot point now."

"What kind of drugs?"

"Prescription. They started selling Ritalin, then expanded to include all the anti-ADD medications. You can't keep those enhanced-concentration pills in stock during college finals.

"The first few bottles of Ritalin were prescribed to Michel Gates on the recommendation of his school nurse," she went on. "He was diagnosed just in time. His father had a balloon payment coming up on the mortgage and their savings wouldn't cover it. Either he confided to Yako or Yako got wind of it and turned him. He already had the connections."

"So Yako killed him?"

"It's a theory. Gates was an amateur, Yako the one with mob ties. Probably Gates got scared and posed a liability. But the Ukrainians are taking a lot of heat right now over our shaky relations with Mother Russia, so his own people took him out before he could be busted for Gates and turn state's evidence. The whole crime community caught paranoia after Whitey Bulger."

I said, "Gates's wife said he seemed to be drifting away from her."

"Now we know why."

"It's so tidy it stinks."

"I'd feel the same way if I were still with the department; a season with Al-Qaeda will cure you of that. Those boys put together a conspiracy like a Swiss watch, and organized crime is always on the lookout for new ways to crook the system. My hunch? Gates's moonlighting is why Amelie doesn't want you asking her son any questions. Wives are tough to fool. Kids are even tougher."

"Too bad they didn't have a dog. We could pencil him into the conspiracy."

"He started by selling his son's prescription," she said. "Those billboards? Donald says 'You know who killed me'? Maybe it was a dead man talking to his son."

■ ■ ■ ■

I dropped the cigarette and twisted it out under a toe. "That's quite a leap just because the boy said, 'I guess so' when I asked him if he wanted me to find out who murdered his dad."

"The obvious answer is usually the best," she said. "The investigation's been trending this way a while. We had to know what you knew before we handed it back to the locals. If we were wrong, and you stumbled into TSA business, we'd have to debrief."

"So you're leaving it there."

"It wasn't a big enough operation for Drug Enforcement. Thank God." Her smile was bitter. "One of the reasons I jumped ship to Washington is I wanted to get away from homicide. The Gates case was no way to finish out the old year."

"Where's this leave Ataman?"

"He ran down a witness who could connect Yako to the Gates kill. On the other hand, we haven't been able to establish a definite link between a man who happens to have a Ukrainian name and the mob. When we cast around outside the area, the board lit up with priors for Grand Theft Auto, including two convictions, the last for five years in Illinois. A car thief isn't the kind of citizen who hangs around after he runs someone over."

"That's one tall coincidence." But I kept hearing Barry say he couldn't find a Boris Ataman in the mob playbook.

"They happen. We'll keep posted; but officially Ray Henty gets it back. Amelie likely told you the truth when she said she didn't want to involve her son any further. How much she knows, or just suspects, is up to the lieutenant to find out."

Somewhere in the building a metal file drawer shut with a boom. "She's missing a bet. Ten grand's good seed toward a college fund."

"The faster you can get the church to cancel that offer, the faster the case gets closed. That's why you're moonlighting for the sheriff's department, isn't it, to run down all the phony leads so they don't have to?"

I didn't answer. That reward was getting to be as unpopular as thirty pieces of silver.

Twenty-Seven

"When does this go public?" I asked.

"Not for a while. We're monitoring it, like I said. The problem with a working hypothesis is it has a way of throwing you a curve. After what happened with the IRS and the NSA, everyone in intel's doing the Lambada to avoid stepping in a warm steamy cow chip in front of an audience."

I started downstairs. "Let me know when it goes to the network."

"Just for your own satisfaction?"

I kept going. "Professional reasons. Until it's Gates was a pusher, Yako shot him, and the Cossacks made Yako's bed for him, all packed up and ready to ship to CNN, I'm monitoring the situation."

She stayed where she was, lifting her voice. "Damn you, Walker. You think I *want* you in Gitmo?"

I couldn't think of a punch line for that, so I turned at the next landing and took the stairs to the street.

With my hand on the fire door I hesitated. Something Thaler had said made my neck itch, but it was gone before I could scratch it.

The tidy way the screenplay laid out wasn't the only thing I didn't like about it. It didn't explain why Rich Perlberg had lied about how well Gates and Chuck Swingline got along. Casting around for a handy lie, his gaze had happened to fall upon a stapler that shared the Indian's name. And there were at least one too many Ukrainians in the frame for the composition. Even in a melting pot like Detroit, you can go months at a time without running into one; when you can't turn a corner without bumping into somebody doing the Saber Dance, the pot's overflowing.

I hadn't eaten at the Blue Heron. The cold air and all that running around was burning calories. My appetite was returning from its long vacation.

There was still a crowd awaiting tables in the Hockeytown Café, so I put in my name and had a beer at the bar while last night's game with Toronto scraped and thumped on TV monitors and a harried typographer struggled to keep up with a panel of sportscasters doing a live broadcast on closed-caption. The poor sap added some new words to the vocabulary but spelled one Russian name right, probably by accident. When the Red Sea parted and a table opened up I sat under a monitor and ate a burger smothered in sauces containing the colors of the Italian flag, washed it down with another beer, and tried to think of anything but the screwball case I'd landed this time.

The crowd cheered every Red Wing goal as if it weren't put up in a jar. I didn't hear my cell ring. When I looked at the screen, I had two missed calls, both placed from the same number. I settled the bill and called Florence Melville back on the sidewalk in front of the restaurant, turning away from a double-bottom truck hauling a load of out-of-tune pianos and sticking my finger in the ear on that side.

"Good news," she said.

The most frightening two-word sentence in the language, after "It's malignant."

"Shoot."

"Our donor called ten minutes ago, withdrawing the reward for Don Gates's murderer. It wasn't anything I did or said," she added quickly. "The call just came in, without explanation. Impatience, probably, over no progress."

"Uh-huh."

"So that simplifies things, doesn't it?"

"Uh-huh."

"I'll lead off my daily church blog with the announcement. I suppose the sheriff's department will take its own measures to make it public. There should be a steep drop-off in bogus leads."

"Uh-huh."

I heard a noise on her end: the rumble and squeak of a carpet sweeper scraping lint off the carpet runner in Christ Church; or maybe just ambient air stirring around her cavernous office. "You don't seem very interested," she said.

"No, it's great. I'm just talking to you on a noisy street. Thanks, Reverend."

Waiting for the car to warm up I drummed my fingers on the wheel. But it was too easy to talk myself out of what needed to be done, so I stopped thinking and drove.

The friendly female party-store clerk took down a carton of Winstons and rang it up along with the rest of my purchases: chips, pretzels, a box of energy bars, four bottles of water, two apples, wet wipes, toothpaste, toothbrush, mouthwash, a can of Barbasol, and a package of disposable razors. "Going hiking?"

"Looks like it." I paid her and lugged the sack out to the car.

I hadn't staked out a place in nearly a year. As an afterthought I checked the trunk. The empty Folger's can was there, with a snap-on lid. I put it on the floor on the passenger's side, and now I was good for what I hoped was the duration.

It was the second time I'd been to church that day, and I hadn't spent one second in a pew. Christ Episcopal stood calm as moonlight, its spires outlined sharply against an oyster-colored sky. There were a few cars in the little parking lot. Florence Melville's was easy to spot, a boxy Ford Flex with a crucifix embossed on the license plate: That would let her park in handicap slots and loading zones while she made house calls of a spiritual nature. I found a space in the far corner and backed into it. From there I had a clear view of the Flex.

There's nothing more uncertain in the work than a stakeout. You almost never know what you're looking for, an incriminating destination, a clandestine meeting, or just a suspicious break in the routine. You don't know how long it will take, hours or days or weeks, so you stock up and see to the immediate sanitary needs. You keep your passport current and handy in the glove compartment just in case you have to cross into Canada — or Mexico, for that matter — an up-to-date atlas on the backseat, a Scotsman's purse full of change for tolls, a roll of bills for bribes and other incidentals tucked in a Kleenex box. I carry a credit card I've never used, and a speed-loader in a Vernor's can with a screw lid.

You take inventory of all that, and then you sit. On the passenger's side, so it looks like you're waiting for the driver. You sit, you watch, you smoke, you listen. Doors open, doors close. Cars pull into the lot, cars pull out. A pigeon pecks at the ants crawling over a box from Wendy's. A hole opens in the overcast, lighter-colored clouds drifting from one side of it to the other, morphing into different shapes, a celestial Rorschach. Doors open, doors close. The radio squawks for a few minutes, just to keep you alert; too long and you start to listen to it. A blowhard talks about the president, an avant-garde saxophonist abuses a noble instrument, a giddy weatherman talks about pressures and fronts, another blowhard talks about the president, a hip-hop group sings an ode to cunnilingus. An ambulance howls and hoots and bleats and wah-wahs down a distant street. Doors open, doors close. A chirp close to your ear makes you jump, and the woman parked next to you opens her door, stares your way for a moment, then gets in and drives away. Cars pull in, cars pull out. A medivac copter with jet boosters churns up the air overhead, low enough to rattle your windows. Brakes screech, a horn blasts. (Light's yellow, moron!) You reach behind your neck and pat the hairs back into place. Doors open, doors close. Your lids are heavy as sash weights and it's the middle of the day. You crack a window to let smoke out and cold air in, splash some bottled water into your palm and dash it in your face, take a sip — a little one, so you don't have to use the coffee can until it's absolutely essential. Cars pull in, cars pull out. You eat an apple. The crunch makes you wide awake, so you crank up the window. People pay attention to open windows in freezing weather.

From time to time you start the engine and let the heater run long enough to clear out the chill, and to keep the engine from getting too cold. You do it every fifteen minutes, which gives you something to look forward to.

You think about your life. Then you stop, because that leads to asking why you're sitting on a buttful of dead nerves in a car parked next to a church. You'll have an epiphany if you're not careful.

Doors open, doors close. A commercial jingle sneaks into your head and you try to sing it on out, but it's burrowed in like a tick and if you pull at it the head will stay in and fester and you're stuck with a kid singing the same chorus out of tune forever.

Cars pull in, cars pull out. You get out for a stretch and find out you've borrowed someone else's feet. Stamp, stamp. A tingle. You put your hands on your hips and arch your back, but nothing pops. You windmill your arms a couple of times and sit back down and slam the door.

And the day wanes.

The clouds were nearly black now, ponderous with the weight of the snow they held. The sun was below them, reflecting off their bellies, a torchiere effect and eerie, as if it were shining up from below. That always brought a sense of nameless anxiety, of something building toward something bad. The big red front door opened and the Reverend Melville came out.

She was dressed for the cold, but not in the sexless heavy-duty gear she'd worn to shovel snow. Her black hair with its silver streak was gathered under one of those fuzzy white flowerpots and a green belted coat hung to the tops of fur-trimmed boots. She'd wound a red scarf around her neck and had a red mitten on one hand, holding its mate while she shook loose a ring of keys. The wind was stiffening; she bowed her head into it, hurried down the steps and across the lot to the Flex, started the motor, and let it warm up while she wriggled her bare hand into the other mitten. She turned on her lights and wound out into the street. I started the Cutlass and followed. It felt good to be going somewhere, even if it was just to her house followed by another long session of the same, and on one of the coldest nights of the year. In the work, you take all the pleasure you can out of the little things.

We drove west to Telegraph, then north. She turned into a strip mall, scampered into a florist's shop with a spectacular show of roses, peonies, and poppies looking like orange crepe in the lighted window. Ten minutes later she came out carrying a multicolored bouquet in a small basket covered with cellophane. I backed out of a space in front of a pet-grooming parlor and turned onto Telegraph a couple of beats behind the Flex. Traffic was heavy with commuters in a hurry to get home to a beer, a fight with the spouse and kids, a late night, an early morning, and the same day all over again. She was a careful driver but an aggressive one, changing lanes approaching stoplights in favor of the one with fewer cars between her and the intersection, and timed her speed to catch most of the lights on the green; either that, or God changed them for her.

Despite all the changes locally, ice crystals trickled down my spine when we entered the Iroquois Heights city limits. I felt like a Jewish refugee going back to Germany for something he'd left behind in 1939.

I'd flipped the rearview mirror to nightside when she turned into a narrow drive with an iron fence on each side and a brass-embossed sign nested in a slumbering flower-bed reading:

HENRY GLADWIN
MEMORIAL CEMETERY

Gladwin had been the commander of Fort Detroit when Chief Pontiac laid siege in 1763. If the town disliked Indians that much, it seemed easier just to change its name.

I idled at the curb for a minute. A cemetery drive is a lonely place every day but Memorial Day, and you tended to notice your fellow visitors. I poked a butt out the window and turned in. A hundred yards ahead shone a pair of taillights, which stayed the same distance as I crept forward, then brightened when the brakes came on. I cruised fifty feet, then took the first turnoff and stopped a few yards in, cutting the motor and the lights.

I spent a lot of time twisting the focus wheel on the binoculars I kept in my trunk and squinting through the gloom to make out her substantial silhouette in the gathering dusk, carrying what I assumed to be the spray of flowers. I'm still saving up for night goggles and a rocketship to the moon. She stopped at a grave, crossed herself, stooped, straightened minus the basket, crossed herself again, and went back to her car.

I ditched the binoculars, slid under the wheel, and waited while she turned into a side path and made her way back to the state highway. By the time I got to the grave, it was dark enough to need the flash. I slid the switch and pointed the beam at the headstone, red marble with a bronze plaque:

DONALD WARWICK GATES
b. 1976

LOVING HUSBAND AND FATHER
"GOD'S FINGER TOUCHED HIM AND
HE SLEPT"

Date of death was problematic, given which side of midnight New Year's Day it had taken place.

There was nothing in it. No law prohibited a pastor from honoring a friend and supporter of the church. There was nothing in it, except friends and church supporters died every day; old lovers less often.

Twenty-Eight

Barry met me at the door of his apartment downtown. He had on plaid pajama pants and a Louisville Slugger in one hand. The titanium shaft of his utilitarian prosthesis stuck out the bottom of one leg. His other foot wore a big ugly black oxford.

"You need to talk to your tailor," I said.

"You need not to wake people up in the middle of the night. You know how many home invasions started with somebody getting his toes stomped on?" He slid the bat into an umbrella stand. I hadn't seen one of those in years.

"It's six thirty P.M.," I said.

"Not in Aspen. You couldn't call?"

"You didn't answer."

"Right. I turned off all my phones."

I told him what I needed.

"Tall order," he said. "I need to know what she looks like."

"The church must have a Web site."

He sat down in front of a flat-screen monitor on an L-shaped desk. His connection was first-rate: He had the Christ Episcopal Church's site in no time, and scrolled down a stack of smiling faces until he came to Florence Melville's, a good likeness.

"I like that hair streak," he said. "Makes things less difficult."

He was faster on the keys than most people who had all ten fingers. I watched a lot of sped-up images whiz past: people entering and exiting shopping malls, restaurants, hotels, walking on sidewalks. Security footage. I asked him how he got the stuff.

"The owner of the Blue Heron isn't the only person I've done favors for. You never know when some drug lord who's been deported to Sicily might walk into the local Seven-Eleven."

"Didn't the feds catch a Nazi war criminal that way?"

"September before last, in Southfield. It was my call."

"Branching out?"

"I should try and compete with the Israelis. Bread on the waters, for when I need Washington."

His eyes never left the screen. Mine did; watching someone surf the Net is like watching grass grow. The apartment was sparsely furnished, no sofa or TV set, no decoration, not even his Pulitzer. When Sam the Butcher came calling, all Barry had to grab on the way out was a toothbrush.

"Hello."

I turned back. He'd freeze-framed on a full-length shot of a man and woman standing in a plush lobby of some kind. The woman was Florence Melville, caught in the act of removing a pair of sunglasses and looking over one shoulder. The white streak in her hair was prominent. She wore a lightweight dress with half sleeves. The man had on a short-sleeved sportshirt and pleated slacks. A time stamp flickered in the lower right corner: 3:57 P.M. 7/8/12.

"Hilton Garden Inn, downtown," Barry said. "They're waiting for the elevator."

"The man's face is blurred."

"Sec." He tapped a key. The image moved. He tapped again, freezing it.

I held my breath. It couldn't be that easy.

"Can you zoom in?"

Tappity-tap-tap. Donald Gates's mild, slightly pudgy face filled the screen.

"Could be a church benefit," I said. "Even a lady pastor prefers an escort."

"Know in a minute." He stroked the mouse. Rows of square stills came up on-screen. He clicked on one, and now we were looking down at a steeper angle at a carpeted hallway with numbered doors on both sides. The couple, dressed as before, scampered down it at accelerated speed. They stopped in front of one of the doors. Gates swiped a key card through a slot, opened the door, held it for Melville, and followed her inside. I caught a glimpse of a sleek bureau and the corner of a snugly made bed.

"Hotel room's a funny place for an auction," Barry said. "Things have come to a sorry pass when a man can't step out on his wife without winding up on a reality show."

"Melville told me they dated before he met Amelie. She sort of left out just when they stopped."

"She wouldn't be the first clergyperson to break the Sixth Commandment."

"Seems a harsh trade for breaking the Seventh." I studied the screen. "Can you print out that last shot showing their faces?"

"Sure. Can I cut myself in, or are you a solo blackmailer?"

"Now, what kind of hell would I be bound for if I tried to shake down a priest?"

"If it's as bad as Detroit, I wouldn't risk it."

"It's just a shock treatment."

"Who for?"

"I haven't worked that out yet. I've been in the dark on this one since the beginning."

"So throw shit on your head and call yourself a mushroom." He loaded a sheet of photo paper into his printer.

"Keep this under your hat, Barry?"

"I might as well. Looks like my Ukrainians sprouted wings and flew out the window."

Twenty-Nine

I crossed the MacArthur Bridge for the fourth time in a couple of days. I was beginning to spend more time on the island than James Scott, and he was a bronze statue standing near the fountain named for him. I forget just who he was, philanthropist or robber baron or just a man with money left over when they put him in the ground. Like the city itself, its history was sliding out from under my feet.

Amelie Gates entered the parking lot while my engine was still cooling, accompanied by a woman I'd seen working the food tent. The other woman had on civilian outerwear like her companion's, but when I opened the window to call out to Amelie the smell of baked beans and onions reached me from twenty feet away. She recognized me — or the car — touched her friend's arm, and left her standing there while she came over.

"I'm sorry you came all this way, Mr.

Walker. I have a ride home."

"I need to talk to you about Don."

"Not tonight, please. It's been a trying day. One of the people we're trying to help threw a fit and dumped over the warming table. Island security Tased him, but not in time. Our best cook was taken to Detroit General with third-degree burns."

"You know what they say about good deeds. I wouldn't bother you, except I think the case is breaking wide open."

She frowned, showing middle-age for the first time in the wan sunlight. After a beat she nodded and went back to her friend. The woman glanced my way — suspiciously, I thought, but after a few years you don't expect to get any other kind — then shook loose a set of keys and veered toward a red Escalade with frozen slush on the rocker panels. I got out in time to hold the door for my passenger.

I left the car in park and twisted in the seat to face her. The picture Barry had printed out was in a manila envelope on the backseat; I could see it from the corner of my eye.

"What have you found out?" she asked.

"Couple of questions first."

"You can't talk to Michel." She raised her chin.

"We're past that — maybe. Was your husband faithful?"

Her head snapped back as if she'd been slapped. "What?"

"I'm not accusing you, although it's a possibility. A love triangle adds more than three sides to a murder case."

"Where are you getting this?"

I said nothing. I could still see the manila envelope.

"Mr. Walker, my husband wasn't perfect, but he'd never have done anything to hurt our family."

I looked from one of her pupils to the other. "Okay. I had to know if you suspected anything."

"There was nothing to suspect."

"Did you and Don have money trouble?"

A tight little smile drove the angry flush from her features.

"He always said the only people who don't worry about money are those who have tons of it and those who don't have a dime."

"I mean serious debt. Is your house mortgaged?"

"Yes, but the payments are reasonable."

"Did you see the papers?"

"I signed them."

"Did you read them?"

"Well, not in detail. Don had. He explained the conditions."

"Did he mention the balloon payment?"

Her eyes flickered. "I don't —"

"No one does except bankers. It had to be dumbed down for me the first time I heard of it. In order to get the lowest possible rate, you agree to pay off a substantial part of the loan in one future payment. It's usually a whopper. Sometimes the entire remaining principal."

"Sounds like a fool's paradise."

"Was Don a fool?"

She shifted positions to face me full-on. "Just what are you suggesting?"

"I'm speculating, not suggesting. A sudden hit to the pocketbook can play hell with someone's sense of right and wrong."

"You're saying he was involved in something illegal, and that's why he was killed."

"He was killed because of something. Why not money?" I forced myself not to look at the envelope on the backseat. I needed it for shock value.

"Who told you there was a balloon payment?"

"I can't tell you that."

"Well, there wasn't."

"How do you know, if you didn't read the documents?"

"I don't know much about such things,

but doesn't it make sense the bank would offer that option near the *end* of the loan, instead of at the beginning? I mean, anyone would have to be worse than a fool to agree to such an expense just to save money for two years."

"Who said anything about two years?"

Her eyes remained on mine. "We refinanced year before last, when the rates were at rock bottom. That's when we signed the papers."

I said nothing.

"Whoever told you that story was lying," she said. "I can prove it just by producing those documents. They're in a safety deposit box at the bank; not the same bank that's holding the mortgage. Don made a point of that." She shook her head. "No, Mr. Walker. My husband had his faults, but being a fool wasn't one of them. And he never committed a crime."

After a moment I faced the wheel. "Okay." I put the car in gear.

She didn't stir. "That's all you have to say, 'okay'? After calling a good man who can't defend himself a cheat and a crook?"

"I got a bum steer. I get more of those than the other kind."

I drove her home without further conversation. In her driveway she got out and slammed the door. She never looked back. I backed into the street with the photo still in the envelope.

The woman who answered the phone in the federal building told me Deputy Marshal Thaler had gone home for the day. She wouldn't give me her home number and her cell wasn't answering.

Someone was lying. It wasn't Amelie Gates. Only a stone psychopath could lie without her pupils changing size. Or a government spook trained by experts.

Florence Melville would have some answers. But I'd retraced enough of my own footsteps for one day. I made a meal out of my survivalist rations and rented a movie, a lobotomy job about a bunch of grown-up frat boys trying to get laid. I laughed my head off and turned in.

I slept late enough to eat lunch for breakfast. I called downtown. A different woman said Deputy Marshal Thaler wasn't in that day. I didn't think I was so important she was ducking me; she'd just have another plausible story to substitute for the one she'd sold me, and an equally plausible story to explain why she'd lied. Trying to brace a cop, any kind of cop, is like playing a shell game when you know there's no pea.

Today's tail was a burgundy Trailblazer. There would be room in the back for a parabolic microphone and whatever other toys they'd drawn from the company chest. By now she knew I'd spoken with the widow, but unless the tech team had found a way around Barry Stackpole's state-of-next-year's-art scramblers, she didn't know what I had on the Reverend Melville.

For once I was ahead of her. I planned to keep it that way.

The guy was good, blending in and out of traffic and giving me as much as a block when the lights were right. I tried shaking him twice, the first time using a city bus for a blind, the second cutting across the site of a demolished crack house bumper-deep in weeds. He stayed on me without visible panic. There were two heads in the car, so parking and ducking into a building and out the back way wasn't an option; the passenger would get out and follow me on foot while the driver staked out the Cutlass in case I circled back.

When I finally lost him it was almost by accident. A DPW crew was digging a tunnel to China on Mound Road, leaving only one lane open. I caught the signalman just as he was turning his sign from SLOW to

STOP. I started to slow down, then gunned it.

"... Cocksucker!"

The signalman at the other end had already turned his sign around and a panel truck had started to ease forward heading toward me; I tickled its front left fender swerving around it. The man holding the sign had to step back to keep from getting clipped by my right side mirror. He, too, had an opinion on my sexual preference; but by then I was free from surveillance.

Not counting satellites, radar guns, and cameras on street corners. Privacy's as dead as Wild Bill.

Thirty

"You're getting to be more faithful than most of the congregation," Florence Melville said.

I didn't jump nearly as high as the belfry. I'd been striding down the center aisle between the rows of pews, intent on the rectory, when she spoke. The acoustics at Christ Episcopal were perfect; she might have been whispering in my ear. I turned and slid my hands nonchalantly into my pockets while my heart dribbled down to a steady beat. She was seated sideways in one of the pews with her ankles crossed, a breviary or whatever spread open on her lap. It was a casual day: blue pullover, black pleated slacks, flat heels. She'd taken off her gold-framed glasses and twirled them in one hand by a bow.

"Hiding from the devout?" I asked.

"This time of day I like to do my reading here. The stained-glass is cheerful in the east light. For some reason it's more mellow than the afternoon sun coming from the west."

She was right. Pink and green triangles and octagons fell across her, making the pale streak in her hair stand out.

"Mysterious ways," I said. "Got a minute?"

"Sure." She closed the book and folded her hands on the cover.

"Someplace less public than Comerica Park."

She lifted her brows, got up, and led me to the rectory. Dust motes did arabesques in the beam slanting in through the east window. "Is this an occasion for brandy?"

I said, "Help yourself. I've been hitting it a little hard lately."

She tilted a palm and sat behind the desk. I didn't sit. I drew the manila envelope, folded lengthwise, from the deep inside pocket of my overcoat and laid it on her calendar pad.

She looked at it, pushing out her lower lip. She stirred, lifted the flap, drew out the picture Barry had printed out. Her face paled a little.

"Where — ?" She looked up at me.

"Big Brother's got cousins all over." I sat down then. "I'm listening."

She laid the photo facedown on the envelope.

"I told you we dated. I may not have been entirely forthcoming about the level of our intimacy. My position —"

I reached inside my shirt pocket, unfolded an inch-wide strip of photo paper, and stretched it between my hands. "Time-stamp. I own a paper cutter. This was dated last July. It's your hard luck the Hilton Garden Inn doesn't recycle its videos as often as some hotels."

She nodded, took air deep into her lungs. It came shuddering out. Then she looked me square in the eyes. "I said before you don't shock easily. Everyone falls from grace sometime. It started after the Independence Day charity auction. Amelie couldn't make it. I was born on the Fourth, just like George M. Cohan. It was my fortieth birthday. Do you know the odds of a forty-year-old woman — and a priest — finding her soulmate?"

"I don't gamble. Where were you New Year's Eve?"

She fell back against the back of her throne. "You can't mean that."

I said nothing.

She flushed, glanced toward the bright window, nodded again, looked at me. "I always deliver a New Year's Day sermon. For me, it's the fourth most important religious event, after Easter, Christmas, and Epiphany: a new beginning, a fresh start, a global baptism, dating to the birth of Jesus. I was here in the rectory, working on it. Midnight came and went without my notice."

"Can anyone verify that?"

"No." Her eyes turned hard as shale. "Why would I kill Donald? He was gentle with me; it had been so long —" Something glittered against gray stone.

"Your position, remember?"

"It was just that one time. The auction was a great success; it means a trip to the Holy Land for our Sunday schoolers. I invited him here for a brandy. Brandy turned into a trip to the Hilton. Other people's private business is your business, I don't have to tell you the rest, except we regretted it right away and agreed never to do it again. I even suggested he and Amelie go to another church, but he said he couldn't think of any excuse that would pass muster with her. I never saw him again except at services.

"I'm a bad priest," she said. "I'm a bad priest, and a weak woman, but I'm no murderer."

"Did you put up that reward yourself, to muddy up the investigation? Maybe not to cover up the murder, but to keep it from working its way around to you and Gates?"

A Bible stood on her desk among some religious tracts, propped up by a pair of brass fish. She slid it out, laid it down faceup, and spread her right hand on it. "No. I couldn't afford it even if I'd wanted to."

"Who did?"

She held the position so long I thought for a second her heart had stopped. Finally she withdrew the hand. Nodded a third time.

I'd scratched that itch I'd felt in the stairwell in the McNamara Building. I had it now, all the pieces; it was just a matter of fitting them together without forcing them. I went to the office to start.

Every once in a while, a fly gets confused and lands in the dish of honey I call my reception room. Richard Perlberg was standing in front of the framed *Casablanca* poster. He wore a checked flannel shirt, corduroys, and snowmobile boots with Velcro closures. An old polar coat and earflapped cap, checked also, hung on the clothes tree.

"This an original?"
"So they tell me. I bought it in a junk shop for ten bucks."
"It's got the year and production number in the lower left-hand corner; that's a giveaway. I used to be a collector. You know what it's worth?"
"More than ten bucks."
"It should be under lock and key."
"Then I'd worry about it all the time. The local talent never steals anything out in the open, unless they can turn it into scrap money. How was the fishing?"
"Shitty. Too much sun up north. The bastards can see you through the ice."
I unlocked the door to the confessional and held it for him. He went in and looked around. "I started out in an office just like this. Hope I never have to go back."
I sat behind the desk and lit a cigarette. He circled the room, glancing at the faux Navajo rug, the filing cases that fell off the back of the *Santa Maria,* the books in the case, some of them accidental collectors' items, Custer fighting Indians on the wall. When the tour finished he sat down a little too hard on the customer chair. "Ouch!"
"Sorry about that. Mouse ate the cushion. You look like a man who could be talked into a drink."

He looked at the clock, but the battery had died at some six-ten in the twentieth century. A smile crept across his open face. His light tan stopped where the cap had left off on his balding head. "That deliberate?"

"If you have to make an appointment to get drunk, nobody told me."

"Join me? They say drinking alone's a bad sign. But poor old Rudy Johnson didn't care who was watching."

I broke out the jug of Old Smuggler and filled two relatively clean glasses. "No ice. There's some snow on the windowsill, but I wouldn't recommend it in this town."

"Neat's fine." He picked one up and we clinked. The first sip of the morning tasted so good I let the rest of it sit. "Peggy told me you stopped by the office. I think I know why."

"Give it a shot."

He turned his glass around in the wet ring on the desk. "You figured out I made up that story about Don and Chuck being buddies."

"You're lucky Chuck's name wasn't Pitney Bowes. I'd've jumped all over that."

He went deeper into the Scotch, but he wasn't ready yet. "Figure out who killed Don?"

"You do it?"

"No. God, no! I was afraid you'd think that when you found out about the dumb thing I did."

"Then no," I lied.

He leaned forward, cupping his hands around the glass as if to warm them. "Gosh, am I stupid. I do a stupid thing and I think I learned from it and then I go and do something even more stupid."

"So you're stupid. You can still run for mayor."

"I panicked, brother. I was afraid if you found out about the stupid thing I did — the first time, I mean — you'd make me a suspect. Suspects in murder cases have a way of getting onto the news. A thing like that can play hell when you're in a position of trust."

I decided to get mad.

"I'm sick of people with positions. Everybody's got one, sitting, standing, lying down. It's the people who keep talking about it I can't stomach. Spill, if that's what you came down here for. Otherwise, pick up your rod and reel and skedaddle."

"Jesus. Who stepped on your tail?"

I let out my breath. I didn't know I'd been holding it. "Only everybody in the damn world since I opened for business. Go ahead; in your own time." I sat back, squeaking the swivel.

"I made a play for Amelie."

"I admire your taste."

"It isn't what you think. Well, not everything you're probably thinking. My wife died. Thirty years old, in perfectly good health, everyone thought. Even her doctor gave her a clean bill of health during her last physical. We went to bed early one night. In the morning she was ice cold. Aneurysm, the coroner said. A bubble broke in her brain. She'd complained about a headache and then she was dead.

"Amelie was especially sweet. We didn't know each other very well; it was a surprise to everyone when she and Don married. She was just the nice girl whose father ran the hunting lodge where we went every elk season. But she came to the visitation — Don was working that night, some computer emergency downtown — and she saw I was in a bad way. She sat holding my hands an hour after we were alone with Elizabeth in the casket. I kissed her."

"Not unusual."

"On the mouth."

"She's French."

"I held it a little too long. She pushed me away. I tried to apologize, but she snatched up her purse and left. She and Don didn't come to the funeral next day."

"Did she tell Don?"

"I don't know. Somehow, I don't think so. Maybe she made some excuse that kept them both away. But I've lived with this thing for two years. When you came around asking about Don and the rest of us in that camp, I sicced you on Chuck Swingline. I didn't think you'd ever be able to find him up there in Canada. He didn't think much of people. I don't know if it had to do with being an Indian or that was his excuse or he was just an antisocial son of a bitch, but I figured when you gave up looking for him I'd be in the clear. So that was the other stupid thing I did."

"I've seen stupider."

He started to lift the glass again, then set it back down and straightened in his chair. "It's important you don't think I'm that kind of a guy. My emotions were all snarled up. I joined a grief-counseling group the next day. I'm still going. They've helped a lot. In fact" — he smiled again, and this time it seemed genuine — "I met someone there. We're taking things slow, but I've made up my mind. I'm going to ask her as soon as I think she won't take it for a rescue operation."

"Okay."

"Okay what? That's a word that can mean a lot of things. If it's 'okay,' okay. If it's 'give me time to think before I turn you over to the law,' it's something else."

"It's just 'okay,' okay?"

His face shut down. "All right, brother. So you want me to twist in the wind. Maybe I deserve it. On the other hand, maybe you're just a callous son of a bitch who never did anything he was sorry for."

"Where were you New Year's Eve?"

"Playing euchre with my in-laws, if you can still call them that. It's been a tradition since I was married; Elizabeth always said it was the most dangerous night to be on the roads. The party broke up after midnight. They'll tell you the same thing."

"Where'd you play?"

"My place in Centerline."

"Last I checked, the time of death hadn't been pinpointed an hour either side of midnight. You could still be on the hook."

"What's my motive? There was no struggle, I heard on the news, so it wasn't like I killed an angry husband in self-defense."

"And brought a gun just in case; no plea there. A desperate cop might say you took drastic measures to protect your reputation." I turned my glass inside its own circle.

The wood already looked like the Olympic flag. "You're wrong, Mr. Perlberg. At least about the part where I never did anything I was sorry for. I've had plenty of practice. You never killed anyone. As far as I'm concerned, you're not even guilty of an indiscretion. What you said stays here." I got up and held out my hand.

He kept his seat a moment longer, then stood and took it. "Somehow I believe you. I —"

"Don't thank me. I'm saving being a callous son of a bitch for the one who killed Don Gates."

Thirty-One

After he left, I gave myself a sobriety test, pouring my Scotch back into the bottle. I didn't spill a drop. I looked at my watch, to no purpose, then picked up the phone, called the Iroquois Heights substation, and asked for Ray Henty's extension.

"Walker, Ray. Anything doing?"

"We're pulling in known area dealers in prescription drugs, with the stress on the ones that specialize in Ritalin and all its cousins. With the Ukrainians out of the picture, we're treating it like a routine drug killing. What about your end?"

"Christ Church dropped the reward offer."

A lung emptied of breath. "Thank you, Jesus."

"Anything new from the M.E. on time of death?"

"There's just one heat register in the basement, and it was shut, probably to conserve energy. You could hang meat down there. That alters the body temperature cooling rate, which for all these new whirligigs in criminal science is still the industry standard. The state police lab in Lansing played with it for six weeks and it came up inconclusive. Screws up the end date on Gates's obituary, even the year, it being New Year's. Why ask? The tips will slow to a trickle now. Thank you for your service to the county. We'll send you a check first of next month."

"Thanks. I'm still on a mission from God."

"Man, you're going to hell."

"Seen it. I had an out-of-body experience once. It looked a lot like Iroquois Heights." I worked the plunger and dialed another number.

"What?" said the voice on the other end.

"We need to meet."

"About what?"

"Tell you when we meet."

"Where?"

I said where.

"When?"

"Eight P.M."

"Why not now?"

"I'm jammed. Christ Church and the sheriff's department aren't my only clients."

"I thought those were the terms of your case."

"Everybody moonlights. Ask any cop."

"Eight it is."

I'd lied. I didn't have any other clients. I wanted to meet after dark, to cut down on innocent bystanders.

I worked the plunger again, called Detroit Homicide. A tired-sounding voice said John Alderdyce was out and asked if it was urgent.

"It is."

The phone rang while I was inspecting the Chief's Special for moths.

"It better be damn urgent," Alderdyce said. "I'm up to my elbows in a drive-by."

I gave him the particulars. In the pause that followed I heard a caster squeak and a door shut. Another squeak, then: "Awfully early to start drinking, isn't it?"

"John, I never felt like I needed one more. I gave you what I got. If it sums up any other way, I'll go on the wagon for good and glad to do it."

"What do you need?"

I told him.

"Holy shit."

"I couldn't agree more."

"Well, hell. I'm past my thirty. The wife'll

be tickled pink to see me take up flower arranging."

After dark, Hart Civic Center was well-lit, a bright space in a helicopter shot that looked like New Orleans after Hurricane Katrina. Lacy ice bordered the Detroit River, with the buildings of Windsor sparkling on the Canadian side. The stiff wind had blown all the potential pedestrians into their heated condos and cardboard packing cases. Choppy waves shaped like cake knives caught the light on their points.

I was dressed for the weather, in a quilted insulated coat, knitted watch cap pulled down over my ears, thermals under my slacks, felted boots on my feet; but I kept walking, stamping from time to time to wake up the vessels in my toes. When I turned into the wind, my own breath froze on my face. I circled the Noguchi fountain, which when it was in operation made a spectacular downward-gushing display, but since some scrap rat with testicles the size of melons had stripped it of copper plumbing — in a public place, shouting distance from Police Headquarters — it was just a stainless-steel ring that looked like the burner on a gas stove. Another Noguchi design, a twisted pylon 120 feet tall, towered at the foot of Woodward Avenue, and Joe Louis's muscular forearm shook its bronze fist at Ontario.

I walked back and forth past Joe Louis Arena, where the Red Wings played, at a little over forty years old crumbling worse than the Coliseum in Rome. The plaza was ten acres of concrete poured on top of a century of oil spills and car radiators, but sinking at the rate of inches annually. The hulk of Cobo Hall, home of the auto and boat shows and the occasional Kid Rock concert, had all the charm of a parking structure that night, and little more when it was in use. I don't know what's happened to local architecture since Albert Kahn hung up his drawing pencils, but if three decades of corruption and municipal bankruptcy didn't finish the place off, some MIT graduate with a compass and protractor would.

I heard a cry of animal pain; an urban coyote caught in a trap? No, just an air horn bent by the wind. An ore carrier or a garbage scow steamed toward Lake Erie, a black blot with running lights fore and aft and a dim glow in the pilothouse. I put the revolver back in my pocket and kneaded my bare hand with the other in a glove to stop it from shaking. I returned the hand to the pocket to keep it warm. A finger wrapped in even the thinnest material fitted clumsily into a trigger guard.

I was wired. Check that; I was scared as hell. It took all the adrenaline connected with the crux of a case to keep me from running back to my car. All that experience, all those instincts, and I hoped I was wrong.

John Alderdyce had in his thirty. I had that in and more, but arranging flowers held no interest, even if I'd put enough aside to buy a vase. The hours were long and the pay was small. The pension plan was worse.

Well, Walker, what did you expect, a banquet and a gold watch?

What I had was a pint of peppermint schnapps. In a warm house it rotted your fillings, but at thirty degrees a swig lit a hearth fire in the pit of your stomach that radiated out to all the extremities and set the tips of your ears ablaze. I took a swig and felt a little better.

"God, I hate this climate."

The voice coming from my back should have made me jump, like the blast from the air horn; but that was before the schnapps. I turned around with my hands in my pockets and said, "Where do we live?"

Mary Ann Thaler was coming my way, hands in pockets also. She wore the same tan calf-length coat, floppy red hat, and ankle boots she'd had on in Yuri Yako's apartment. I had no reason to think the little bulge in the right pocket belonged to a pint of anything but Glock Nine.

"I was hoping to get an assignment in Central America," she said, "holding the hand of a material witness in a car bombing. My section chief acted like he was doing me a favor by letting me stay in my hometown." She stopped a few yards away. "You wouldn't have another drop in that flask, by any chance?"

I drew out the flat bottle and tossed it underhand. Her left hand, clad in a red mitten, swept out of its pocket and caught it. A crease broke the smooth white line of her brow when she read the label.

"Try to keep an open mind," I said. "Even Walker Blue tastes like WD-forty at this temperature."

She untwisted the cap, tipped up the bottle, shook herself; frowned, shrugged, took a healthy swig. She recapped it and tossed it back. I caught it in my left hand. Just a couple of southpaws that night. "You're right. Not bad."

"I picked up the habit hunting deer. Every time I took a nip, I saw another twelve-pointer." I pocketed it without helping myself a second time. A man needs what wits he has.

She made a half-turn to look at the river. Clouds billowed from her mouth when she spoke. "You forget how beautiful this town is, in places. They tell me this was all warehouses before I was born. Tearing them down and replacing them must have meant jobs for a lot of people."

"About as many as lost theirs. You can hide a lot of graft under a few thousand tons of steel and cement." I didn't turn with her. She'd put her body between me and that right-hand pocket.

"Not you and me, though. If the world weren't wicked we wouldn't be working."

I grinned. The air froze my gums on contact. "Be vewy, vewy quiet. I'm hunting wabbits!"

She turned back, and both hands were still in their pockets. I relaxed my grip a little on the Smith & Wesson. "That was a slick piece of work today. I had the day team on you."

"Don't put them in front of a firing squad. I had a little help from the DPW. I didn't spot the tail tonight."

"There wasn't any. I knew where you were going. You told me, remember?"

"I wasn't sure you'd go along with it. Those unbugged fire stairs being so handy."

"It isn't good to make such things a habit.

Sooner or later somebody gets a bright idea and goes back to RadioShack."

She stopped talking, waiting for me to ask her to the prom. I didn't ask. The little crease reappeared.

"I heard about the reward," she said. "How'd you manage it?"

"I didn't. But you knew that. You withdrew it. Why not? You're the one who offered it in the first place."

Thirty-Two

She didn't say anything. Her face didn't change. I'd have been disappointed in her if it had. It would have been a shame to throw away the best poker face I'd ever seen.

"I'd like a look at that Justice Department application sometime," I said. "I bet it reads like Lewis Carroll. The best con man in the world wouldn't score better than sixty. Only a psychopath could ace it. You post a fat fee for information leading to a murder conviction, knowing it'll just bring every crackpot and get-rich-quick bum out from under his rock and gum up the works. It's practically a guarantee the investigation won't lead to the murderer."

"Just for the sake of argument, how would I get my hands on ten thousand dollars?"

"You didn't have to. No one would ever collect. Yuri Yako looked good for a while; you made sure of that by having Roy Thompson overhear him threatening

Gates's life. Or did you? Roy can't back it up or deny it, being a grease spot in a hit-and-run."

"My, my. I'm just a little Lucrezia Borgia. What else you got?"

"An embarrassment of riches. First, you tried to pin Gates's murder on the Ukrainian mob, but when that started to peter out you loaded his computer with incriminating drug traffic. With all that and the distraction of treasure hunters calling in tips, you turned an ordinary homicide probe into a Chinese box so complicated it made the Kennedy assassination look like a slam-dunk."

"And I did this why?"

"I'm still working on that. Right now I'm wondering how much of this you farmed out and how much of it was DIY."

A shoe sole scraped concrete; that close to the river it sounded three feet away. A figure in a black hoodie took another step off Jefferson Avenue, spotted us, hesitated, turned, and wandered back the way he'd come, casual as any fresh-air fiend. He had a bundle under one arm, probably filled with tools.

"Came back for the rest of the fountain," Thaler said. "This is what I left behind. I don't miss it. But I did miss the part where you said you had proof."

"Boris Ataman."

She said nothing. The lights might have been turned off for all I could read of her expression.

"I don't know what you offered him," I said; "maybe a chance to sweep his record clean. These days, the feds have a lot more authority over the locals. My guess is you went down the list of known offenders at the wheel until you came across one that sounded Ukrainian. But you should have cross-checked it with RICO, because as it turned out he wasn't connected. That's when that thread ran out."

She moved a shoulder. My hand tightened on the revolver; but it was just a shrug. "Felons break on the witness stand," she said. "If that's all you got —" She turned toward the street.

"Did I say that? I've got another witness who can tie you to that reward offer. She's an Episcopal priest. They don't break so easy. The rest is just legwork: cracking Gates's so-called drug connection, to start.

"Both witnesses are in protective custody," I added; "in case you were worried."

She showed her teeth. "WitSec?"

"Nope. Local. You don't put chickens in a pen owned by the fox.

"It almost worked," I said. "You made two mistakes, not counting the big fat one at the beginning. Just to sweeten the pot, you tried to fob me off on little Michel. You knew about his Ritalin, which I'm guessing is where you got the drug idea, and I told you what he said about finding his father's murderer. His ambivalence. But all he wanted was for it to be over."

"You said two mistakes."

"You said something in that stairwell in the federal building that bothered me. You said, 'The Gates case was no way to finish out the old year.' But the cops couldn't fix time of death either side of midnight in that chilly basement. Only his killer would know he died before the new year."

She turned her head, said something under her breath that made a jet of bitter vapor. She looked back at me. "Are you wearing a wire?"

"No. You can check me, but please make it quick. I don't handle the cold as well as I used to."

She stepped closer then, fixed her eyes on mine. She shook her head. She could read pupils too. "Go for a walk?"

"Sure."

We took the walkway along the river, just two friends out for a stroll, chins tucked into their chests against the cold. The lights of the Ambassador Bridge were strung like pearls in a black void. Cars crawled over it, a flatbed truck probably carrying steel coils to one of the auto plants. They were only a few blocks away. Another world.

"It doesn't matter now if this goes public," she said. "It did then, which is why people died. We're encouraged to develop individual sources. You can interpret that pretty widely, but I might have strayed a few yards off the reservation.

"I won't go into how I came to select Donald Gates," she continued. "His job, of course, was the first criterion. His church service entered in; he was an earnest do-gooder, ripe for the you-can-help-your-country speech. My idea was to bring those cameras at traffic lights into the national database: which plate numbers kept coming up at which hours near subversive cells. It was a safe way to identify persons of interest without putting a deep-cover op in jeopardy. By now everyone's an expert on the leaks in the system."

"It wasn't such a bad idea," I said, "if you put aside the First and Fourth Amendments."

"We did that years ago. Anyway, Gates didn't have any qualms; I said I picked him well. But then the story broke about NSA surveillance of domestic telephone conversations, that shitstorm, so I pulled the plug. They threw the IRS director under the bus; what chance would a junior deputy marshal have? Only Gates didn't want to stop."

"Why would he? He had a mindless job, and he'd seen too many spy movies."

"The problem was I'd never told my superiors about the operation. Then I made another in my long string of spectacular mistakes: I told Gates it was all my show when I shut it down."

I stopped walking and faced her. "That's like a married man dumping his mistress."

She nodded. She was looking at the river. "They always threaten to tell the wife. I went to his place New Year's Eve to try to talk some sense into him, wave the flag, the greater good. He started to dial nine-one-one."

"So it was a passion killing."

She looked at me. "Even pros panic. They're human. You should know that. I saw your medical record."

"The difference is I was the only one I almost destroyed. You put a car at his house the day before, probably with a parabolic mike; Henty said V-A-L was among the plate numbers blocked out for law enforcement use. You heard the Gates's plans for New Year's Eve. You knew he was going to join her at the party later, and that he'd be in the house alone. If you didn't think your conversation would end in killing, you wouldn't have taken that precaution."

"No. Remember, only he and I knew about our arrangement. I told the surveillance man it was a need-to-know assignment and that the reasons fell above his pay grade. The Service gives you all the vocabulary you need for any situation. I needed to talk to Gates without risking his wife overhearing the conversation."

"You could have done that without laying so much groundwork. He worked alone in that computer room, and there were a half-dozen other places you could have braced him for a quiet talk. His basement in the suburbs was ideal for swallowing a gunshot."

"Shit!" She swept the back of her mittened hand across her eyes. As far as I could see it came away dry. "You know, if I were a man, and not a woman trying to prove she could get along against all that testosterone, I'd've run it past the brass, and they'd give me the go-ahead. They have precedents: RICO, national security. Then when it blew up they'd use the game plan they always use, stirring up dust until it all went away. See, I was still thinking like a city cop."

"What about Yako?"

"He was easy. As a witness under our protection, he had old friends anxious to make contact. One anonymous phone tip, and no more liability."

"He was no loss, but Roy Thompson was just an ordinary Joe who might have testified he never heard Yako threaten to kill Gates. That one was cold-blooded."

"I don't guess I can sell you that one as blind luck, but it was. The locals should have locked Ataman up and broken the key off in the lock the second time they arrested him for Grand Theft Auto and reckless driving. Sooner or later he had to kill someone. It just happened to be Thompson."

"Too thin."

"The Ukrainian connection. I couldn't believe my luck. But that's all it was, blind dumb luck. Roy Thompson just happened to be standing in front of it.

"It wasn't worth killing him," she went on. "Eyewitness testimony? You know how well that stands up during cross. I won't say I wasn't relieved when he was run down, and that it took one more lowlife off the streets; I mean Ataman. But I'm no serial killer. I'd sooner face the music."

I thought about that. It was the one bit of

stupid coincidence every case needed to convince the skeptic. But I bought it like I bought Grand Circus Park. At this point I couldn't believe anything she said.

"What the hell happened to you?"

She looked down at her feet. Kicked an imaginary can.

"I don't know, Amos." She looked up. "That's a lie. I know. I didn't leave the department just because of the opportunity for advancement. I was sick of Detroit. I thought it was the dirtiest, most corrupt place on earth. Then I got to Washington. All those gray little people playing with the fates of ordinary folk like the gods on Olympus."

I fixed on her eyes. "Maybe you didn't go there to kill him. I think you didn't, that you hoped to sway him with words. On the other hand, you didn't go there *not* to kill him. But that's something the defense and prosecution can work out. My job's done."

I saw it then. I'd struck a nerve, like tuning a piano and plucking the key I wanted. Her gun arm tightened.

"Don't," I said.

It made her hesitate. "For old times' sake?"

"For old times' sake, I'm telling you there's a DPD sniper posted on the Joe

Louis roof with a night scope. The second you draw that piece will be your last."

Her eyes flicked that direction, but of course she didn't see anything; not until she looked in my eyes again.

All the air went out of her then. She nodded. "Henderson. John wouldn't go with anyone less. So what now?"

"Walk away. He's got orders only to shoot if you draw your gun.

"You won't get far," I said. "Just far enough so I don't see it."

She turned, her hands still in her pockets, and walked away. I watched the pale back of her long coat until darkness swallowed it. Just at the last second a trick of reflected light bathed her in government green.

Thirty-Three

Ray Henty heard it all without interrupting. He had the cover off the 1966 Fairlane in his carriage house workshop and rubbed at the primer with a chamois cloth, removing dirt and the ragged edges of the original paint until it glowed as pink as a rose. When I finished he broke two cans of Stroh's out of the refrigerator and handed me one.

"The union wants me to run for sheriff," he said, popping the top on his. "I thought about it. I'm still young enough to have some ambition. But it's too close to the top. That's where it all floats."

"You can't retire on an open case. I know you."

"The way you knew Mary Ann Thaler? Thanks, Amos. I should be a good host and let you finish that beer. Right now I can't stand the sight of you."

"It had to be a city man on that roof. You'd have had to ask for cooperation, and that'd be too many who knew."

"You made the same mistake she did."

"I hoped she'd give herself up, plea to Man One. That might not have been on the table after the press got wind of it."

"Bullshit."

"She saved my life a couple of times. Maybe two murders wiped all that out, I don't know."

"I do. They did."

"She might still come in."

He set down his can, picked up the cloth, and went back to rubbing. I put my can down unopened and left.

I'd gotten almost as bad from John Alderdyce the night Mary Ann went missing. He didn't buy my story that she hadn't told me anything anyone could use, but he knew it wasn't worth anything anyway. I'd refused to wear a wire, and he knew as well as I did it wouldn't work. He'd trained her himself. Jack Henderson — "Hawkeye" they called him at 1300 — never asked why he'd been recruited for the job, and on orders from the inspector never told anyone else. Maybe his wife; but any woman who's stayed with a cop fifteen years is as hard to crack as a Navy SEAL.

■ ■ ■ ■

Mary Ann must have been prepared, with a go bag packed, passport and all. When the feds searched her office and apartment, all they found was her service piece. She made it as far as Nova Scotia, where the FBI met her before she could board an international flight. She didn't resist. They tagged her with misappropriation of funds. There might have been something in it, although I doubt she ever thought she'd have to make good on that ten thousand. But they could keep building on that and keep her in Camp Cupcake for twenty years.

Boris Ataman drew life without parole for the hit-and-run killing of Roy Thompson, Yuri Yako's would-be accuser. That story vanished between the six and eleven P.M. reports.

They hung the Yako murder on two brothers named Kobolov, heavy lifters for the Ukrainian mob, who'd gone back to Kiev. Extradition proceedings are pending; Barry keeps me posted on that, not that I care.

Ray Henty left the department six months after our last conversation to take a job as head of security for a national hotel chain. He advertised the Fairlane for sale on

Craigslist. The sheriff promoted Benteen, the detective Henty had inherited from the Iroquois Heights Police Department, to acting lieutenant to fill his post. The poison was rooted too deep in that city to snuff out. It was already wearing through the new coat of paint.

The last time I saw Don Gates's smiling face, it was vanishing behind a sleek gray Lincoln being pasted up in big square sheets to advertise a new dealership. One ear and part of his chin was all that was left.

Somewhere in there my phone rang and a female voice — warm, middle-register — used my first name. My heart made a happy little lurch, as if the past several weeks hadn't happened, like when you dream; but she was in federal custody, not likely to make bail, and in any case wouldn't waste a call on a work-related acquaintance. That's all I was when it came down to the nuts and bolts, never mind that it was one of the longest relationships in my history, marriage included. The caller was an old girlfriend. She had a friend applying for an investigator's job with Reliance, a big firm with offices in Detroit, Birmingham, Chicago, and San Francisco, and he needed as many references as he could get. I told her anything I had to say would only harm his chances. After thirty seconds she agreed. I never heard from her again. I barely remembered her anyway. She'd only remembered me because of the association.

Hanging up, I felt blue. I wanted a drink; but I hadn't had any liquor in the house or office in ten days, hadn't been to a bar, and had swept the medicine cabinet of pills, including a couple of dusty Advils in the bottom of a bottle. I went out for a cup of coffee instead, which turned out to be a mistake. I sleep soundly when I sleep at all, and the caffeine didn't help. I was running out of substances to abuse.

Several times I thought about calling Jeannie Miernik, the therapist in Redford Township, purely for social purposes; but I never got past the first digit. I'd seen too many episodes of *The Sopranos* to think that would work out.

I'd gone straight from Henty's house to Amelie Gates's, where I gave her as much as I thought she could handle; some of it was green-stamped, and she didn't have to know about Florence Melville. She let me talk to Michel then, with her in the room. I told the boy his father had died in defense of his country. That was enough, for ten years old. In a couple of years, when he started asking questions, it would be his mother who would have to answer them. I got the better part of that deal.

ACKNOWLEDGMENTS

I'd like to thank Richard Perlberg and Jeannie Miernik for donating their names to this book in the cause of literacy. Any resemblance beyond those names is purely unintentional.

ABOUT THE AUTHOR

Loren D. Estleman is the author of more than seventy novels. Some of his many honors include four Shamus Awards, five Spur Awards, and three Western Heritage Awards. He lives in Michigan with his wife, author Deborah Morgan.

www.lorenestleman.com

The employees of Thorndike Press hope you have enjoyed this Large Print book. All our Thorndike, Wheeler, and Kennebec Large Print titles are designed for easy reading, and all our books are made to last. Other Thorndike Press Large Print books are available at your library, through selected bookstores, or directly from us.

For information about titles, please call:
(800) 223-1244

or visit our Web site at:
http://gale.cengage.com/thorndike

To share your comments, please write:
Publisher
Thorndike Press
10 Water St., Suite 310
Waterville, ME 04901